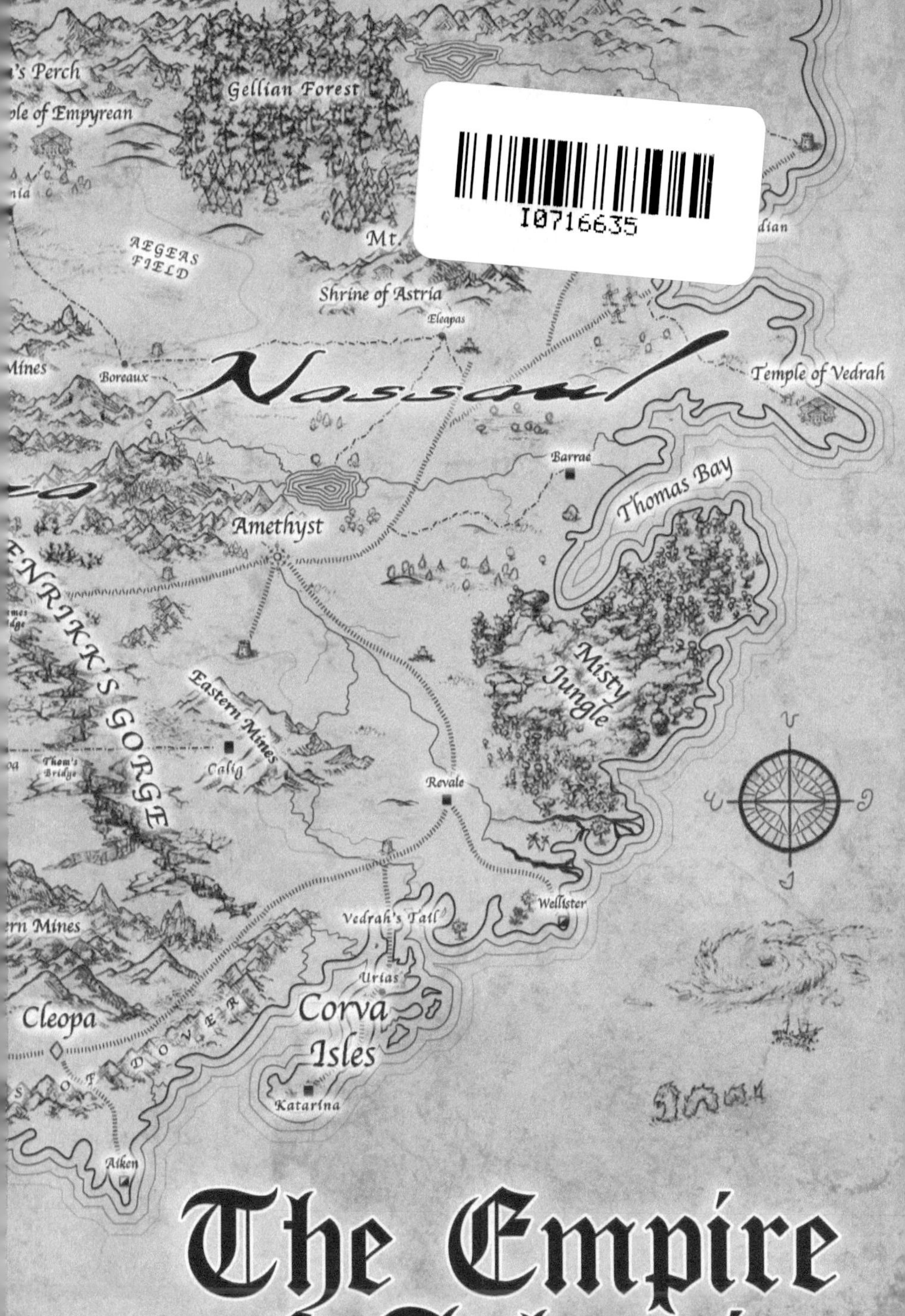

The Empire of Arkania

The Avat Prince

VOLUME SEVEN

ISBN 9781957330112

First Edition Printed August 2021
MVP TV Edition Printed November 2024

Printed by IngramSpark in the USA.

House MVP
16 Thomas Patten Dr., P.O. Box 21
Randolph, MA, 02368

https://www.housemvpmedia.com

The text of this book is set in 12-point Adobe Garamond Pro.

Even when the flames arise, know that you are not alone.

A the Ava-t Prince

VOLUME SEVEN

WRITTEN AND ILLUSTRATED BY

MYRANDA V. PETERSON

THE AVAT PRINCE:
TALES OF ARKANIA

To access locked skits for
THE AVAT PRINCE:

First, get reading!

When you see the word 'TV' at the end of a
sentence, it's time for a skit!

Illustrations are paired off with these pages.
Scan an illustration's QR code to access its skit.

Enter the password.

Enjoy the show!

(Don't forget to come back to keep reading the story!)

MVP
TV

HOUSE MVP

PREVIOUSLY IN
THE AVAT PRINCE...

With leads on Çaru'qu running cold, Brent is forced to refocus on his primary goal of saving the slaves. But, things go awry after his very next mission: half of the slaves he rescues die en route to Taranis.

This rattles Brent, for it's his very first failure. Shortly afterward, he learns that Renée and her mother, Terra, are in the throes of battle in the sparring hall. Apparently, Terra offered Renée an ultimatum: defeat her in a match, or give up on training.

Renée rises to the challenge. Victorious, she visits the slaves that survived Brent's mission and learns how horrible her enemy truly is.

That same night, Brent experiences another vision of a blue-haired man trapped in a realm of light and mist. But, he still doesn't know who the man is. Elsewhere, Terra agrees to share a secret technique with Renée to ensure her success as a raider.

In the Empire, Viceroy Diomedes is forced to make a statement denouncing the rumors that claim Skylok is a member of the royal family. But he is conflicted, for it may very well be that these rumors are true...and the reason for Skylok's exile still haunts him as much as it haunts Brent. Later, he receives troubling intel about Orinn and is given a chilling message with it: "the Shade has entered Lyrik."

Back in Taranis, the villagers celebrate the graduation of Renée and her fellow classmates. But right before the ceremony, Brent is drawn away by an apparition of a man in a frightening mask, and learns that Xëri may have a connection with these figures. After failing to get the truth out of her Brent opts for speaking with retired councilman Qëmzhi in the hopes of securing more information. Perhaps his knowledge of Taranis' founding and the enigmatic 'Elder' will give him insight into these strange visitors...

Elsewhere, Emperor Koberius learns that Skylok could very well be the same person that he once tried to kill as a young ruler.

It infuriates him. And Empyrean is just as angry.

50

BRENT WASN'T ABLE to visit Councilman Qëmzhi for at least another few days, the reason being that the old man had recently caught a bad summer cold and had been bedridden the entire time. He hadn't even been able to attend the Feast of Liberty.

At last, shortly after his recovery, Greta went to visit her old friend. She casually shared the news about it over lunch with Lilian and Liam.

The intel scout had then relayed the information to Brent, who'd taken it upon himself to visit the elderly man on his own. Seeing as he'd just gotten over his illness and was suffering from a drop in his overall mental capacity, he reasoned that going alone would be the best thing to do. After all, he didn't want to overwhelm him.

"Sooner you go the better," Liam told him. "Greta said he's only ever got a short window where he can make conversation."

"Got it."

Despite his declining mental health Councilman Qëmzhi had been a sprightly man once, during the early days of Taranis. At least, that's what Brent had heard.

He'd been deep in his senior years even back then, but he'd still had a head of wavy, red hair that he'd often worn in a loose braid that hung down his back. His eyes, full of light, had glittered whenever he spoke, and his laughter had been contagious.

Shortly before Brent's arrival in the village, Chief Ivan had notified everyone that the councilman would be stepping down. The news had come as a bit of a shock to many, although others had deduced that it had only been a matter of time. After all, in spite of his jovial demeanor and pleasant outlook, Councilman Qëmzhi was certainly beginning to show signs of mental disability, as he could no longer articulate his thoughts without veering off on some sort of unrelated tangent, or abruptly wondering after the strangest of things while in the middle of conversation.

Nevertheless he'd received a rather joyous send-off, with the Main House's kitchen staff putting together an extravagant meal of flame-roasted doranis, stuffed proardea, buttered yams and seared vegetables, along with all manner of desserts and cold juices, some of which had been fermented for the older party-goers. Pennant banners and signs were hung up, and for the entire day the village had been in the throes of what was almost a second annual Feast.

The old man's retirement had further gifted him with a large, private room in one of the older apartments, where the walls had been given extra insulation to minimize outside noise, and the wall windows faced the sun, so that warm light could always filter inside. At night thick curtains could be drawn over them, to keep the chilly air at bay.

He'd also been given a fresher bed and cozy furniture, but for some reason the elderly gentleman preferred to sleep near the windows on a padded, roll-up mattress. Apparently, it made him feel "more at home".

Normally, he came out often and sat with the older villagers often, engaging them with idle words and board games that they sometimes shared with younger tenants of the apartment structure. He always walked with a staff, its head all knobby and fitted with a jade stone and golden rings, and his scarlet hair had grayed completely. His beard had lengthened, dangling towards his navel, and the proud shape that he'd borne in his youth had hunched over and shrunk. Truth be told, he'd lost at least a good foot-and-a-half of his height since he'd retired.

According to Greta, he was usually in better spirits at around midday into the early evening, and would usually begin to show symptoms of his waning intelligence just a few hours before bedtime.

But of course, for him, bedtime was rather early: just a bit before sunset in fact. He also took at least three naps everyday, which made finding a decent time to talk with him that much more elusive.

But Brent wasn't keen on losing this fight. Thus did he secure a bowl of bass stew from the Main House's kitchens and make his way down to the northern apartments.

The corridors were quiet, and he knocked before going into the man's room.

"*Xaivu,*" came the councilman's wobbling answer.

"*Çiçuvëi çiraçu.*" Keeping to Aionbo, Brent twisted the knob and entered.

Councilman Qëmzhi was already sitting on his sleeping mat by the window, with the sun's late afternoon light pouring right onto him.

He was certainly a tiny thing these days, at least half Brent's size, with wispy gray hair that was stained with faint reminders of red. Liver spots dotted his balding crown and his pointy ears were long; at the end of his right ear, there was a silver ring with a decorated feather hanging off of it.

"Oh! *Burën-çam!*" He greeted the raider delightedly and waved him over. "To what do I owe this pleasure? It's not everyday you get paid a visit from one of the chief's sons." His eyebrows rose when Brent sat in front of him. "Ah! You brought me dinner!"

"Yep! Fresh from the Main House's kitchen." Brent set the bowl of chunky stew on the standing tray that was right beside them. "Heard you just got over a cold. Eklaire says this kind of broth is great for that."

Qëmzhi laughed and clapped his hands together. "Oh, and I'm sure she would be the expert on that sort of thing! Thank you, boy. I'm certainly quite famished right about now!"

Taking up the spoon that had come with the dish, he started on his meal.

He smacked his lips. "Mm, it tastes like the Feast!"

"Well, we did have it at this year's Feast," Brent said. "Tasted so good that people keep requesting it from the Main House."

"Ah! The Feast this year! Oh, that reminds me, Renée was supposed to graduate this year, yes?" Qëmzhi slurped up some of his meal and looked at Brent with wide, dark eyes that were blurring with failing sight. "Has she?"

Brent grinned. "Yep! Along with the rest of her class."

"Ah, good, good! Good to see Terra let her graduate. So fast, you young ones grow up so fast…"

Slurrrrrp.

"Actually, there *is* something I wanted to ask you, councilman," Brent admitted, leaning against the window frame. The hot sun warmed his skin. "It's about Taranis. And about how the Liberation Fronts got started. I have to, uh," he scratched the back of his head, "give a lecture as a stand-in at the schoolhouse tomorrow."

"Mm, yes." The old man slurped some his stew. "Go on."

"Well…how *did* it all start?" Brent sat up. "Xëri and the head council talk about someone called the 'Elder' a lot, too. Does he have family here? Did he help build the village?"

Qëmzhi froze.

Brent noticed, but he chose to wait and see how the old man would respond.

"Hmm…" Qëmzhi lowered his spoon. His dark eyes went up, down, and all around —

Anywhere but to Brent.

"Can't say," he said at last and he took more of his stew. "Can't say, I'm afraid. We're not supposed to share about the Elder, not the Elder…need to keep that under wraps, keep his daughter safe."

"Keep his daughter safe? Safe from what?"

"Can't say, I'm afraid. I'm afraid I can't say more."

Brent tried a new angle.

"I met someone who mentioned her," he said. "A guy wearing a mask that looked like a lion. I think he was an aetheriest."

Qëmzhi paused again.

This time, he looked into Brent's face intently. "You saw a Shade?"

"I…" Brent blanked. "A what?"

"Hm, strange…" The old man stared into his soup. "They usually keep to the shadows…never show themselves. Order has strict rules. Did the Elder change the rules?"

"Order?" Brent frowned and sought to press him for more answers. "Wait, what're you talking about? What Order?"

"The *Order, Burën-çam,* the Order! They watch over us, don't you remember? That was part of the deal."

"Deal? What deal? With who?"

"With the *Order* boy. By the Elder's charge. Couldn't have built Taranis without it, especially since the Empire's so dangerous these days. Emperor's so dangerous these days."

Brent frowned.

It seemed as if the old man's mind was slipping away already. Sensing that he only had so much time left before he was completely gone, Brent decided to focus on gaining intel about the only other issue that had been plaguing his thoughts.

"…Councilman," he started, "do you know anything about a place that's filled with green and gold mist?"

"Green and gold mist?" The old man looked up at him, his soupy spoon hovering an inch away from his mouth.

"I've seen it a couple of times." Brent frowned distantly as he remembered the sight. "There was always someone there: a man with blue hair whose face I can't see. The last time I saw him, I think he saw me, too."

"Ohh!" Qëmzhi looked at him and then gestured to his head. "You have blue hair."

"R-right," Brent tried smiling. "But he's not me. I thought you might know something?"

"Hm…trapped…"

"What?"

"Hm…" The old man stirred his soup idly. "Yes. Yes, I believe there was one story, when I was a boy…a legend about a man locked…no, sealed. No, he was away…away, *somewhere,* he…hm." The old man frowned.

At length, he peered up at Brent, who was watching him anxiously.

"You have blue hair."

The sides of Brent's mouth twitched dryly. "Everyday."

"Strange…I've never seen any other Avat with blue hair before…but there were stories…when I was a boy. A legend about a man sealed away *somewhere*…"

"Right." Brent tried to catch the man's eye. "You mentioned that. So what story was —"

Without warning, Qëmzhi grabbed his shoulders.

"Dragons! And *serpents!*" he whispered frantically, and he squeezed Brent's shoulders until his knuckles turned white. "Dragons and serpents!"

"Wh-what?"

"Yes, dragons! And serpents! A story from when I was a boy, yes…" He glanced away and up again, then looked all around. "Can you see them? Dragons and serpents?!"

"Dragons and…see them? See them where?"

"Yes, the dragons and the serpents, they were on the isle, yes, yes…be wary of the dragon, the dragon's wish…dragon's wish… that's why we needed the Order to protect us. The dragon hates the Order, and the Elder's daughter leads them…needed to keep her safe, to keep us safe. Because she wanted to keep the Avat people safe…keep everyone safe from the dragon…and the man locked away, he…yes…" The old man touched his wrinkly forehead and then frowned distractedly. "He was picked to fight the dragons and the serpents, once. Only people like him could do it, because they were picked. He was picked, you know. I think he had blue hair."

Looking up at Brent, he did a double-take and stared at his hair. "You have blue hair." He paused and stared in wonder at Brent's sky-colored tresses. "That's interesting."

Brent stared back at him, waiting for him to go on.

"Anyway." Qëmzhi waved a hand, thought for a second, and then went back to eating his stew. In between bites he went on babbling about nothing: the soup's flavor, the heat, and how it made him quite warm and grateful. There was no more talk of dragons and serpents, nor even further mention of the man that Brent had witnessed. It was as if the discussion had been wiped from the aging man's memory altogether.

Evidently, his medicine for the day was wearing off.

But Brent wanted to try again.

"Councilman," he said, touching the man's shoulder. *"Councilman.* What legend? Is there a story about the man who's sealed away?"

"Oh, yes, everybody knows the story of Zion." Qëmzhi waved his hand away. "But no one knows where he is. I think he died. Mother said the same. He had blue hair, I think."

"Zion…like the Hero, Zion." Brent paused, seeming to consider whether or not he should entertain the concept. At last, he just sighed. "That's just a story, councilman. About an Avat aetherian. They don't exist, remember?"

"Hm. Do they? Can't say, I'm afraid." He blew on his soup before slurping up more of it. "Elder said I shouldn't say…part of being on the head council. Elder's rules. Have to keep the daughter safe. But I can't say…wait…"

He stopped.

Brent watched him again, waiting.

"I think I forgot my staff."

All of a sudden, the old man got to his feet and started for the door.

Out of the side of his eye, Brent noticed that Qëmzhi's staff was leaning against the wall, right behind where he'd been sitting.

"Councilman —" Rising, he touched the man's shoulder.

"Dragons and serpents!" the man exploded, and Brent lurched back in shock. "The dragon's wish! The dragon's wish is why he was picked, yes. He had to save us but he was sealed, he had to be sealed but he was saved…"

"Councilman —"

"Dragon's wish…hm…that's what mother used to say, yes… dragon was dangerous, yes, Empire's dangerous…"

Locking his hands behind his hips, the man shuffled over to the door and left, muttering all the while.

Behind him, Brent both looked and felt even more confused than he'd ever been.

"Anything?"

That was the first thing Aaron asked when he saw Brent walking through the northern apartments' front yard. Liam was with him, a pair of wild hen slung over his shoulder. They were fresh kills.

"Went about as well as I thought it would." Brent joined them amidst the buzzing of the village, with people going to and fro without much care or trouble. "But he did share something."

He relayed to them a short summary of the councilman's ramblings.

"Sounds like he's talking about *The Third Aether War*," Aaron concluded.

"It's just a story," Liam reminded him. "Zion the Hero, an Avat aetherian, goes to battle against the imperial gods Empyrean and Vedrah. In the end he wins, and seals them both away."

"It almost sounds like that other legend that Pops brought up before," Brent said quietly, his mind clearly elsewhere. "Now that I think about it…"

"You mean about that supposed third imperial god that those masked guys kept mentioning?" Aaron recalled. "Çaru'qu."

"Yeah." Brent looked at him. "The plays we did at the schoolhouse always told the story about Zion the Hero defeating Empyrean and Vedrah in some great battle. But Pops said there's a story about Çaru'qu doing the same thing. Biggest difference here is that Councilman Qëmzhi made it sound like Zion is still out there somewhere."

"What, like he's the guy you keep seeing in that weird dream?" Aaron cocked an eyebrow.

"Don't know."

"That stuff about the Elder's daughter and the Order gave us something to work off of, at least," Liam admitted.

"Right. So the Elder that the head council keeps mentioning made some kind of deal with them, where they weren't allowed to share anything about him or his daughter in order to protect her from some 'dragon'." Aaron folded his arms. "As for the guys in masks, they keep popping up near us because, by the Elder's charge, they're supposed to help protect his daughter and us from that same dragon."

"Still doesn't explain anything about what that guy told us back in Cleopa," Brent said. "Councilman Qëmzhi didn't mention anything about someone named 'Çaru'qu'. He just kept comparing me to Zion because apparently he had blue hair just like I did. Still, at least we know one thing." He started away.

"What's that?" Aaron watched him go, his crossed arms lowering.

"Now we know why Pops and Xëri weren't all that worried when we mentioned those masked aetheriests." Stopping, Brent turned to look back at them. "Apparently, they made some kind of deal with them that goes back to when Taranis was built."

"What're you gonna do then?"

"For now, nothing." Brent was resolute. His decision on this was final. "But this stuff about Zion…that's where I need answers."

⤙ ✵ ⤚

At the sound of Renée's cry and the landing of an inhuman kick the evergreen tilted, filling the evening air with the creak of splintering wood. At last, it tumbled to the earth with a devastating crash that shook the ground.

Somewhere, birds took off.

With her hair settling across her back as her quintessence returned to her, Renée caught her breath. Standing upright, she exhaled deeply and looked over her work.

The tree was some eight or nine stories high and was about several feet in diameter. On its collapse, it had crushed a number of shrubs and vegetation, along with one or two smaller trees.

Turning around, she faced her mother.

Clouds inched across the tawny skyline, freeing the setting sun's light so that Terra's cross-armed figure was caught in it.

She smiled faintly. "Well done."

Renée beamed.

⤙ ✵ ⤚

Teal and golden mist floated before Brent's eyes, revolving around him as a gentle cloud. The world was mirrored beneath his feet, creating even a perfect reflection of himself, and the sky was filled with light.

It was warm, all around. And the air hummed quietly, all around.

The blue-haired man appeared before him again, his back still to the visitor. His hair swirled in undulating waves, his long bangs hid his face, and he smiled at something that Brent couldn't see.

Slowly, he turned his head, and Brent caught the shortest glimpse of his eyes: they mirrored this world of green and gold, or perhaps were filled with it.

A decorated feather hung from a silver ring in his right ear —

His pointy *ear —*

Brent woke up.

He was lying across a table in the Main House's archives. Filled with journals and logs that recorded historic missions that had been led by Taranis' fighting forces, it was the closest thing that the village had to a library. Albeit a somewhat autobiographical one.

Lifting his head, Brent looked around.

The table was covered with documents that he'd scanned and pored over the previous night. What with dawn peeking over the windowsills, he guessed that he'd fallen asleep at some point.

Dropping his head, he raked a hand through his hair.

The archive hadn't told him much.

Another dead-end.

Disappointed he cleaned his workspace, only to soon feel a shiver run down his nape. Whipping around, he looked outside.

Nothing was there.

Or… was that a shadow just beyond the windowpane, in the shape of a man?

He stepped closer, cautiously, slowly, eyes narrowed. There was definitely *something* standing there —

Just outside of the library, someone fell over with a shout.

"You all right?" And just like that Brent was gone, a blur rushing to assist.

And so when Oruviçu became visible, he looked after the raider with his hidden, aetherial eyes in silent contemplation.

51

WHEN HE REACHED the crown of the hill that inclined away from the sparring hall, Tyre stopped and stretched his arms high over his head.

"Man, what a boring, sunny day!" he gasped when he finished. The day was indeed that: sunny and boring.

The Feast of Liberty had come and gone, bringing with it the long-awaited graduation of Renée and her full induction into the auction raiders. No raids had been assigned to her or any of her fellow graduates, though. In fact, in the weeks that had followed the Feast there seemed to be a standstill in all of the raiders' rotations, the cycle having ceased ever since the last round of scouts had yet to return to the village. From what Tyre understood their numbers even included Aizen, the same scout that had reported the holiday slave caravan that had gone through Heletica's Pass.

As a result of this, the warriors in Taranis had been dispatched to handle all sorts of tasks around the village instead, from assisting in hunter-gathering to recovering villagers who'd reportedly been wounded by wild animals out west. Other times, they were recruited to track down pests and thieving creatures that had wandered in from the mountains.

Some villagers, like the healer Khirsta, even requested ingredients for medicines or recipes that couldn't be grown in the village. As simple as those jobs sounded they always wound up being the hardest, because at some point it involved fighting a bloodthirsty animal or traversing dangerous caves and mountainsides.

Tyre had participated in many of these odd jobs, as had Renée, a fact that he really only knew because of Kro's interest in her daily doings. Despite having yet been given an official imperial assignment, she seemed to be handling her temporarily restricted responsibilities with humility and skill.

Tyre wasn't particularly bothered by the new change in routine. While he certainly appreciated his work as an auction raider, he had to say he preferred the liveliness and community of the people of Taranis over the snobby imperials any day. Even his days in the Aether Circus were ones he didn't like to remember.

But at the same time, he wondered if he should be upset by the change. He'd only been living in Taranis for so long, but he couldn't shake the sense that things weren't supposed to be running this way.

Unless the slave traders were taking a break.

Did they do that?

Either way, he sort of felt like he was getting rusty. Sure he still trained, but attacking dummies in a field wasn't the same as a life-or-death battle against soldiers and slave traders with the lives of innocents hanging in the balance.

He wondered if he was getting complacent.

"You should be basking in these slow days!" an Avat man said to him from a nearby home, having heard the boy's remark. He was working in a small garden with two little Arkanian girls. "You might never get another chance like this again!"

"Yeah, I know," Tyre replied courteously, and he waved to the girls when they greeted him. "I just wish that *something'd* happen, y'know?"

He and everyone else on the road jumped out of their skin when something in Harver's workshop exploded. A small addition that Jeffrey had had some of the builders add to the side of his house for her some time ago — after she'd decided to become an engineer and showed much promise in it — it actually shook with the detonation. Black smoke curled out of the windows.

Tyre rounded on it, for it was practically right behind him.

His eyes bulged. *"Harver!"* he exclaimed, and he rushed for the door.

Other villagers looked on in frenzied concern.

Someone else just shrugged. "Eh, this happens every other week or so."

Throwing the door open Tyre meant to charge inside, only to stop short when a wave of smoke crashed into him.

He backed away, coughing. Then, joining the aether, he sent a gale rushing inside.

Papers flew everywhere and as the smoke cleared, he saw Harver coughing and swatting at the air within.

"Stop it, stop it!" she hacked. She kept one hand pressed to her thighs to keep her skirt from flying around. "You're making a mess!"

"It's already a mess!" Tyre retracted the wind anyway and everything that had been blowing about settled back to the floor.

Harver's workshop was indeed a mess. The floor and counters were cluttered with labeled drawings and sketches, as well as half-finished instruments, dismembered gadgets and shelves of older and failed experiments.

A strange mechanism was sitting on a table against the back wall, which was scorched, and a thin veil of smog was spewing out of it. Dented metal that had been warped by the explosion made up its inner assemblage, and a long steering handle was attached to it.

"Are you okay?" Tyre asked, daring to step forward. When his foot crushed some crumpled pieces of parchment, he stooped to gather them up. "What the heck happened?"

"It's just...wrong!" Harver threw her hands at her smoking contraption before she ruffled her hair in anger. "And of all the worst-case scenarios, it exploded!"

"Yeah..." Tyre finished picking up the papers and tried to examine one. It was cluttered with notes, diagrams and strange doodles that he guessed were meant to express their creator's more complicated ideas. "I can see that."

"I've been working on this since last year and still nothing..." Harver sank into the table, her face buried in her arms. "I just want it to float..."

Wary, Tyre carefully navigated her shop and took a peek at what she'd been working on.

He couldn't figure it out. "What is it?"

"It's supposed to be based off of this ancient piece of Avat technology I learned about a while back. But it's just not coming together...everything else is fine but, I think there's just *one thing* missing..."

"Whoa..." Tyre looked the object up and down. "I've never seen anything like it! Which reminds me..." He faced her with a slight frown. "The Avat people were known for being inventive, weren't they? And I mean, even the Liberation Fronts get to use crazy gadgets on raids thanks to what you engineers whip up. But... how'd the Empire manage to overthrow them during their expansion?"

Harver snorted. "Everyone knows why."

When Tyre didn't respond, she looked at him. She was surprised by his honestly clueless expression.

"It wasn't that hard for them, I guess." She poked at her instrument. "By then there were already tensions between the Avats and humans. Before he became the founding emperor, Axelius Arkania made truces with some of the Avat tribes. Then he went on his whole 'human supremacy' rampage, tricked them all and turned their own technology against them. After the dust settled, he destroyed all their stuff."

"Why didn't he just keep it?"

"Pride? He didn't wanna accept that Avats could build things that humans had never considered."

"Oh." Tyre frowned. "That's stupid."

"My old master was crazy about their lost technology," she continued quietly. "He was obsessed with it."

"That explains why your inventions are the best!" Tyre said with a grin.

Harver was morbid. "I guess you could say that."

Tyre's face fell and he scratched his head awkwardly.

He'd never been able to put his finger on why it was so, but ever since his arrival in Taranis, he'd been drawn to Harver. Perhaps it was because of her ingenuity, her curiosity about the world and how she was always finding new ways to make the raiders' jobs easier when it came to saving the slaves. Almost all of Taranis' gadgets and tools had crossed her worktable at some point, he'd learned shortly after his first mission, whether she'd been the one to design them or had simply enhanced their efficiency.

After learning that, he'd reckoned that a mind like hers had to be fascinating. And yet, despite their living in the same village, he rarely got to see her because she was always holed up in her shop. Though, her work ethic only made him want to learn more about what she was like.

Now that he was finally faced with a rare opportunity to talk to her, he couldn't help but blurt out one question after another.

Even if he didn't think the whole question through.

"So…did you…like your master, then?" he asked next. When Harver looked at him, he blushed furiously. "I-I mean! Agh, no…" He covered his face with a hand. "That came out wrong…"

Harver's big, dark eyes thoughtfully wandered away.

"I don't remember if I liked him," she said at length, jarring him out of his self-pity. "I don't think I *dis*liked him." She balanced her chin on her forearms and stared at the wall. Several diagrams and reminders were tacked to it. "He taught me how to read and how to write. And how to think critically. He didn't treat me the way most masters should. But he got arrested for it and as part of his punishment, they took me away from him."

"Oh." Tyre's once anxious look softened with empathy. "And that's how you wound up in the slave trade again?"

"Yeah. I'm lucky Jeffrey and his team intercepted the slave traders who had me. They might've killed me otherwise, if they'd found out I'd been learning."

Tyre paused, another question rising to his thoughts. He hoped it wasn't half as stupid as the last one. "D'you think…that you make this sort of stuff as a kind of homage to your old master?"

Harver paused, considering. Standing up, she looked him in the eye with a frown. "No. Why?"

His heart skipped.

"No reason." He shrugged and laid her papers on the desk. "But from what I was taught, the Avats had aetheriests help them make their gadgets sometimes, didn't they? We still do the same thing now, remember? So, maybe I can help you with your…" He gestured to the steaming pile of metal. "Whatchamacallit."

Harver's frown deepened. "I don't need —"

"This is s'posed to float, right?" Tyre interrupted, painfully unaware of her disapproval. Before she could respond, he laid his hand atop her contraption.

His quintessence tickled her cheeks when it rolled out of him, grasping the aether, and to Harver's surprise her mechanism actually began to levitate. It wasn't even half a foot off the table before Tyre spread his palm beneath it, and expelled a burst of wind that gave it the extra lift it needed to hover on its own.

It hung in the air then, drifting up and down as if it were bobbing on an invisible wave.

She stared at it, astonished. Open-mouthed, she looked at Tyre.

He didn't notice, but rather frowned thoughtfully as he considered what he'd done. "Hmm…maybe it'd work better if I gave it the ability to repel the gravitational pull of the planet…but then it wouldn't be able to go very high…" He did a double-take to Harver's wide-eyed look. "What? I picked up a few things since I got here!"

"Tyre…" Harver grabbed his face with both hands and pulled him close, much to his surprise. "You've just given me the greatest idea!" She beamed.

Tyre smiled. "Great!"

Harver didn't let him go.

His face falling, Tyre glanced away. He looked at her again, sheepish. "Um, not that I'm complaining, but…can you let me go now?"

⤙ �— ⤚

"Harver sure is taking her time," Brent said, standing at the bottom of the main road with his two-piece staff strapped to his back. Renée, Liam and Eklaire were with him. Save Eklaire, who only had a small bag belted against her side, they also had their weapons equipped. "From the way Tyre was talking, you'd think she would've been ready by now."

"Maybe she's still getting her things?" Renée dropped onto the flat-faced rock that edged the road and leaned her weight on her arms. "I've seen her get…overly excited when it comes to traveling to Heletia Cavern. She's probably going overboard again."

"She's coming now," Liam said and he shifted to face the village. "She sounds…heavy."

The others looked at him, confused, and they faced the main road in anticipation of Harver's arrival.

Within seconds, Harver emerged from between a pair of houses. In that moment, everyone understood what Liam had been trying to say.

An enormous, animal-hide bag was strapped to her back, and its outer pockets were bulging as it clonked and thumped with every step that she took. She had a shoulder bag on as well and not surprisingly, it, too, was bursting with an uncertain amount of objects. There was even a black hat on her head with a lantern affixed to it. Inside of its glass casing, there was an unlit candle.

While the candle-hat made sense to them, given that they were charged with bringing her into the dim depths of Heletia Cavern, Brent and the others couldn't figure out why she needed everything else.

"Okay!" With the summer sun shining in the clear blue sky she stopped in front of them, beaming like a schoolgirl excited for her first day of class. "I'm ready!"

Brent couldn't keep from laughing. "Harver, there's no way you need to bring your whole workshop with you. We're just going to Heletia Cavern and back."

"This isn't my workshop!" she protested. "This is *necessary.*"
Some of them exchanged looks.

Taking Harver to Heletia Cavern was Brent, Renée and Liam's newest odd job, a task that Liam had inadvertently picked up while collecting vegetables from a farmer. With Heletia being a network of caves from which the villagers acquired material for weapons, jewelry and the engineers' inventions, it was the perfect place to source supplies for her secret invention.

"Okay," Liam had agreed when Tyre had brought the job request to him. "When does she wanna go?"

"Now," the aetheriest had answered meekly.

Liam had stared at him. Then, he'd sighed.

"Uh, she said she'd ask Brent and Aaron, too," Tyre had told him.

"Aaron's away," Liam had replied and he'd started back up the road to Greta's hut, so he could drop off his produce and gather his equipment. "Ren can prob'ly take his place."

"He's away?" Tyre had repeated and he jogged to catch up with him. "Wait, he got to go on a mission? And here I was thinking the scouts had lost touch!"

"Don't know. He might've snuck off again."

"Oh."

"I'll get ready." Liam stopped at the corner of Greta's home once they'd reached it. "We'll meet Harver at the foot of the main road. You coming, too?"

"I told Harver I wanted to." Tyre rubbed the back of his neck guiltily. "But as soon as I said that, Heldar found me and said he has a job for me and a few other aetheriests. We've been getting a lot of wild predators wandering into the western valley, so he's gonna need us to seal off the path they've been using to get in."

"Oh. Better luck next time, I guess." Liam turned to enter the hut.

"Huh? What do you mean by that?"

"When it comes to spending more time with Harver, you might need to be more persistent. Can't always wait for the opportunity to show up."

"Hey — wha — " Tyre had sputtered and his face had grown increasingly red. "Wh-what're you talking about?!"

Liam hadn't elaborated. He'd only smirked before entering Greta's hut and shutting the door.

Eklaire, though not a raider at all, had decided to tag along with the group almost as soon as she'd heard Renée speak of it. The way to the Cavern was known to be relatively safe and what with Brent, Renée and Liam being the escorts, she'd felt assured of her own safety.

"Besides, all work'n no play makes Eklaire a borin' gal!" she'd exclaimed.

None of them had seen very much harm in it.

"Come on, you guys have been with me to Heletia before!" Harver reminded her friends presently, looking between them all. She shifted her weight, making her backpack rustle. "What if I find something there that could be useful for one of the gadgets that we already have? Then I can double-check it right on the spot and make sure the materials are compatible, instead of bringing home a bunch of extra stuff I don't need."

"As opposed to bringin' along a bunch of extra stuff you don't need?" Eklaire teased.

"It makes sense, Eklaire!"

"I don't know, Harver…" Standing, Renée crossed her arms and eyed the gigantic bag concernedly. "Do you even think you'll be able to carry all of that the whole way there? We can't use horses or even saigas for such short travels in case there's an emergency here, so it's going to be almost an hour away on foot."

"Give or take another with all of…" Brent gestured to Harver's backpack. "That."

Harver frowned at him.

He just shrugged, hands spread.

"If she wants to bring it, we should let her," Liam said, turning to the others. "She knows what it takes to gather materials for the engineers more than we do."

"Guess you have a point…" Renée eyed Harver's luggage one last time.

"True enough," Brent agreed.

"You good?" Liam asked as Harver lumbered past him with a contented smile. "I'll help."

"Huh? Oh, no, I'm okay!" She directed her smile to him. "I may be smaller than you guys, but I can totally handle this! I've done it before. Besides, I don't want anyone touching my stuff."

Liam only nodded, but was still uncertain.

"C'mon, we all know how stubborn she is with that." Brent patted Liam's shoulder and started into the valley. "Let's get going!"

"Nooo! Wait for me!"

The group spiraled at the familiar voice, and they watched as

Mekial came running down the hill after them.

"Mekial?" Renée frowned quizzically. "What're you doing here?"

"I just heard that you guys are going to Heletia Cavern! Without *me!*" He slowed and stopped in front of her, panting.

Now that he was closer, she noticed that he had a couple of knives belted to his waist. They were long and thin, similar to the one that their mother used in her own battles. Normally they were made of wood, but in the last few weeks he'd graduated to steel.

"I'm coming, too!" he said.

"You're still a trainee!" Renée reminded him, her hands rising to rest on her hips. "You're not allowed to go on any missions in the valley yet. You're not even old enough to go hunting!"

"Oh, come on!" Mekial stuck his arms out towards Eklaire. "*Eklaire* is going, Ren. And she's not even *in* training!"

Eklaire giggled. "He does got a point."

"Besides, Heletia Cavern is like, the coolest place around!" Mekial spread his arms wide for emphasis. "I can't stay behind!"

"It is pretty neat," Harver admitted quietly, looking at Renée.

Renée turned to Brent, as if his counsel could bring them to a clear decision.

He raised one of his shoulders. "He's not wrong. I mean, if Eklaire can come along I don't see why he can't. We've got his back."

"I even told Mom and Dad!" Mekial piped up. "I'm not sneaking off and breaking the rules! Unlike *some* people." He looked around. "Wait, where's Aaron?"

"Probably snuck off again," Brent shrugged. "Haven't seen him for a few days."

"You sound jealous."

"I'm not." Brent looked away.

Mekial snickered. "Totally jealous."

"I'm not!"

"Okay, okay," Renée returned her attention to Mekial with a soft sigh. "I'm sorry for not saying anything. But if you're going to come along, stay close to me, all right? We don't know what we could run into out there."

"It's just the road to Heletia," Mekial reminded her, leaning his weight onto one foot and pressing his fists into his sides. "We'll be totally fine!"

"That doesn't mean you shouldn't stay alert."

"Right, Madame Fuddy-Duddy."

"Madame Fuddy-Duddy?" she repeated, cocking an eyebrow.

"What? You don't have a cool outlaw name yet. So, I'm giving you a lame one."

He laughed at his sister's expression and before Renée could counter him, a chorus of shouting came to them from a higher part of the main road. Looking towards it, they swiftly pinpointed the source.

Mekial's friends were sprinting down the hill towards them, their faces open in delight as they hollered for the group of older villagers to wait.

Dillon was at the head, his startling green eyes bright with excitement, while close at his heels tagged Klarys and Kurt. Lacey and Lilian weren't too far behind.

Unsurprisingly, Dillon reached the small group first. He stopped short beside Mekial. "No fair, Mek! You ran off before you even finished helping to clean the classroom!"

"I was seizing the moment!" the trainee retorted.

Dillon scowled in the face of Mekial's haughty look, but turned when Renée addressed them.

"All right, let me guess," she sighed, looking them all over. "You guys also heard about where we're going."

"You bet we did!" Dillon replied, his enthusiasm returning. "Take us with you!"

"Yeah, I wanna go to Heletia!" Lilian cried as the others chattered noisily, and she grabbed Liam's leg. "Lemme come!"

Brent smiled crookedly. "We can't take *all* of you."

Lilian swung her face towards him, pouting. "Aw, c'mon!"

"I've never been!" Dillon told him. "I wanna see what it's like!"

"C'mon, Uncle Liam, please?" Lilian begged, setting her dark eyes on her guardian. She tightened her arms around his leg and poured every ounce of effort she had into her wide, pleading stare.

"No, Lil." Calmly, Liam put a hand on her head. He'd long-since overcome her puppy-eyed looks. "We'll be quick. You won't even know we're gone."

"But I already know you're leaving!"

"We really can't come?" Kurt asked dismally, his shoulders dropping. An instant later, his energy returned with a bothered frown. "Is it cuz Mekial took the last spot?!"

"No, it's just that it's like Brent said," Harver replied. "We can't take everyone. Plus, you'll probably just get lost in the caves, and that'll only cause us trouble!"

"But…I really wanted to go…" Lacey's sight began to blur with tears. With her head bowing, her face twitched and her shoulders jumped, indicating she was about to cry.

Seeing this, Harver glanced between her friends, desperate for their help.

"Aw, c'mon, now! Y'can't be cryin' on a sunny day like this!" Eklaire knelt in front of Lacey and swiped her nose with the tip of her finger. "Tell you what: when we get back, I'll tell ya'll all about it! I'll even have Liam act it out for ya!"

Liam frowned. "Why me?"

"Cuz yer great with kids!"

"You are good at telling stories, Uncle Liam." Lilian smiled up at him.

Liam's cheeks turned pink.

"After that, we can all pig out on some sweet snacks!" Eklaire went on to Lacey. "And we'll play fer the rest of the day!"

Lacey perked up at that offer. She sniffed. "We will?"

Eklaire nodded. "Mmhmm!"

Lacey smiled back, her tears gone. "Okay!"

"I *do* like sweets," Kurt admitted thoughtfully, and he smiled when Eklaire tousled his unruly head of hair.

Behind him, Klarys scoffed and folded her arms. "It's not the same as going…"

Next to her, Dillon sulked silently.

"Cheer up, guys!" Brent said, looking to them. "You may not get to come to Heletia this time around, but maybe later we can take you to the training grounds for some archery practice. Those targets could always use another hole or two."

It was Dillon's turn to cheer up then. "Okay!"

"Can I go, too?!" Lilian cried, rounding on her uncle. She was still clutching his leg but had been glancing between everyone while they'd conversed. "Please?! And then you can show me how you shoot and throw at stuff by listening for where they are!"

With a gentle smile, Liam tousled her hair. "Sure."

"Yay!" She hugged him.

Klarys sighed. "I *guess* that sounds fun…" she mumbled, her gaze still averted.

"C'mon, Klarys." Renée tilted a knowing smile towards her. "We all know you're excited."

Embarrassed by the obvious truth, Klarys refused to look at her.

"Okay, so are we done now?" Harver butt in, bouncing on the balls of her feet. "Let's get going already! I don't want it to be too late when we get there!"

"Maybe you should leave yer house behind," Eklaire joked. "All the extra weight could *really* slow us down, y'know."

"Eklaire! We've been through this already!"

"Don't say I didn't warn ya," Eklaire sang.

"I already said I'd be fine!"

"All right! We're going to Heletia!" Mekial cheered, pumping his fists into the air. "The cave of wonders!"

"The cave of great treasures!" Harver called out from behind him.

"Yeah!" He jumped excitedly and ran off, one fist skyward as if to rally the others. "To Heletia!"

"Tooo Heletia!" Brent joined, going after him.

"Heletia-a-a-a-a!" Eklaire shouted, her voice bouncing as she sprinted after them.

Liam went after them and with a bright grin, Renée did the same.

At their backs, Dillon and the others shouted farewells and wishes for safe travels.

"W-w-wait!" Harver sputtered over them, and with great effort she jogged to join the group of friends that were speedily leaving her behind. The contents of her bags jostled noisily as she went. "Don't leave me! I'm the reason we're going!"

No one waited for her.

"Guys…!"

Given the distance between Heletia Cavern and Taranis, the journey there took them just a little under an hour, as Renée had suggested. By the time they reached the hill that sloped down towards it, Harver was huffing beneath the weight of her bags.

She'd pushed through for as long as she could, managing to grit her teeth in a false grin and stubbornly refuse assistance whenever it was offered to her. But, now that they'd nearly reached the end of their journey, she was just about ready to collapse.

With her back hunched she took wide steps along the dirt trail, squatting as she walked so as to better support her luggage. Although her village attire was airy, what with her loose, wide-neck crop top and skirt, sweat was beading on her forehead and she was finding it difficult to breathe.

Smiling sweetly, Eklaire tied her hands behind her waist and leaned down to see Harver's face. "How's it goin' there, Harv? You look like you been rode hard'n hung up wet."

"I'm…fine…" the girl panted, straining to take another step.

"'Scuse me!" Taking advantage of Harver's slowdown, Brent stole her shoulder bag and hat. Swinging the bag onto his own shoulder, he plopped the hat onto his head.

"Hey!" she gasped, her cheeks coloring.

He winked at her and kept walking.

Eklaire giggled. "You looked like you needed the help! But you certainly weren't gonna ask for it. It kinda looks like you could use some help with yer other bag, too —"

She broke off with a yelp when Harver snapped upright.

"No need for that…" she gasped, grinning at what lay ahead. "We've made it!"

Eklaire followed her gaze and sure enough, she saw that they had indeed arrived at Heletia Cavern.

The entrance was a massive, gaping hole that tunneled into the depths of a rocky mountainside, and the sloping, meandering path that the group had been following leveled out at its threshold. On one side of it stood an assembly of tall trees. A small clearing was fixed behind them, bordering a more densely packed part of the forest, and on the other side the grassy hill rolled into the surrounding plains.*tv*

CREEPY-CRAWLIES
CODE: YUCKYBUGS

When he was close to the cave Brent stopped walking, and with one finger he pushed the rim of Harver's hat up in order to see the cave entrance completely. Even from here he could spot a number of strange, glowing flora that were only local to the cavern, and the life of the fields yielded to the rocky path and dead branches that were scattered across the cave floor. In other places, the curious eyes of cave-dwelling creatures blinked at him in interest.

Liam stopped not too far from him. He gazed up at the cave entrance in stoic silence.

"Well don't just stand there, let's go!" Harver shouted as she came nearer. "We're burning daylight!"

"This is gonna be so great!" Mekial jumped up and down and ran into the cave.

"Mekial, be careful!" Renée warned, going after him.

"Don't leave us behind!" Eklaire dodged in after them.

"Hey, wait!" Harver cried as the others hurried into the Cavern next. "I can't run that fast! Guys…!" She groaned and, readjusting her backpack, she trudged in after them.

It wasn't long before the light of day could no longer follow her inside. Still, with her highly sensitive hearing, she could tell that she was catching up to everyone else: the clink of their weapons and their soft footfalls as they followed the Cavern's first winding passage reverberated in the darkness.

"It's pitch-black. I can't see my hand in front of my face!" Mekial finally squeaked.

"Why're you freaking out? You wanted to come!" Renée retorted from within the darkness.

"Can't you turn on Harver's lamp-hat-thing, Brent? Aren't you still wearing it?"

"Aww, poor wittle Mekial is scared!" Brent teased.

"Not everyone has superhuman-hearing that can guide them through a pitch-black cave, okay?!"

"Here, pass me my hat, Brent." Harver stuck her hand out in the direction of his voice and waited for the feeling of her hat to touch her palm.

When it did, she put it on and reached into one of her bag's outer pockets. From it she produced a pair of metal nail guards that were lined with flint. Snapping them over the candlewick she lit it, enclosing everyone in a warm, amber glow that was as powerful as a set of torches.

"Better?" She smiled at Mekial and closed the glass casing over the bright fire within.

He loosened with relief. "Much."

"You were scared," Renée decided.

"Was not!"

"I can hear your heart pounding," Liam said flatly.

Mekial backed down. "Really?"

"Check it out…" Brent ventured to the edge of Harver's light, his head tilted back to view the entirety of the chamber that they were in.

Grand stalactites hung threateningly from the black ceiling, their tips flickering in the light of Harver's hat, and all along the ground fallen rocks lay around craggy stalagmites. What looked like thin ledges lined some of the far walls, winding towards holes that may or may not have lead to other parts of the Cavern, and further away the path that they were on forked into several. Some of them weaved around stalagmites before forming a set of natural staircases, while others descended into lower, unseen places; only one went straight ahead and vanished into the darkness.

"*Echo!*" Mekial suddenly cried, cupping his hands around his mouth, and his voice bounced around them, rebounding between the walls until it softened into quiet.

Liam tilted his head a little, listening to the cave. His eyebrows drew together.

"Sounds like it goes pretty deep —" Renée started.

"*Get down!*" Liam yelled and to her shock, he grabbed her and pulled her to the ground with him.

Not even a split second later a wave of frenzied lukites erupted from the darkness, squeaking shrilly as they flew out of the cave. They were pups, that much was certain, and they tore out of the blackness on dark, webbed wings with flashing fangs and bodies of velvety fur.

Startled, everyone else ducked and covered their heads, falling to their knees as they waited for the nocturnal creatures to pass.

When they were finally gone, Eklaire dropped her arms and looked out after them. "Well, what in the heck were those things all spooked for?!"

"Unexpected company," Renée said and she shot Mekial a disapproving frown as she stood up.

Mekial smiled with a weak, nervous laugh.

"We should be more careful from here on out," Brent said, turning to face where the lukites had come from. "There're all kinds of things living in here." He started towards the only straightforward path.

"Like spiders and beetles and slimy lizards!" Harver added excitedly as she went after him.

"Spiders…?" Renée repeated softly, and she wrapped her arms around herself as she followed.

Thanks to Harver's light it was much easier for them to maneuver their way through the Cavern, and they were able to admire the many different species that they came across. There were bioluminescent mushrooms that stalked the bases of natural pillars and blankets of sparkling moss in one cave, and along another path they caught the shadows of furry creatures that raced away before they could be fully seen.

In still another place, a set of glowing green eyes blinked at them from within the darkness.

Mekial noticed them first. "Um…what is that?" He pointed.

Harver followed his finger. "Oh. Probably a luka."

"You mean an *adult* lukite?!" he whisper-yelled.

"Yep."

"It could eat us!"

"Yep. But it doesn't seem hungry. Even if it was" — she tapped her candle-hat — "they hate any form of light."

"Oh…" Mekial turned back to the piercing, glowing eyes that were still pinned to them from afar.

He could've sworn he heard the creature snarl.

Gulping, he caught up with his sister.

They passed through the remainder of the hidden luka's private chamber and entered a narrow passage that tunneled deeper into the Cavern. Upon emerging, they found themselves to be in the largest part of the caves that they'd entered yet.

The rocky ceiling was vaulted high above their heads and here and there, giant holes opened up to the sky, permitting rays of sunlight to pour in like spotlights. Cliffs, ledges and sloping paths were scattered throughout, and at the very back of the cavity there was a large body of water. One giant beam of light shone upon it, causing its surface to glisten, and all along its underwater walls what looked like shells — thousands of them — shimmered along with it.

To the far right of this a grouping of evergreens could be seen, with some of the tall pines standing on top of cliffs while others were planted at their bases. Boulders, patches of grass, weeds and scraggly-looking bushes surrounded them, and several beams of golden light fell upon the entire area.

Harver approached the edge of the cliff that she and her friends had arrived on and dropped her shoulders, leaving her backpack to slide off and land behind her with a powerful *thud*.

"All right." She planted her hands on her hips. "Here's our stop!"

"Great." Brent moved to join her in looking out over the large cavity. "Where do we start?"

"Today, I need a good pile of shells from that lake," Harver said, pointing at the lake, "then I'm gonna need to check over there" — she indicated the partly forested area — "for rubbershrooms."

Brent narrowed his eyes in confusion. "Rubber…shrooms?"

"Rubbery mushrooms." She faced him, her arm falling. "That's really the best way I can describe them. The area over there's pretty bright already, and because of their color they'll be easy to spot."

"Okay. Good thing there's so many of us…let's split up." He took off Harver's shoulder bag and laid it beside her backpack. "Harver and I'll head over to that lake for some of those shells."

"I wanna go diving for seashells, too!" Mekial piped up.

"Lake shells, Mekial," Brent corrected amusedly.

"Same thing."

"I'll look for the rubbery-mushrooms!" Eklaire exclaimed.

"I'll go with you," Renée said.

"Same," Liam finished.

"All right." Brent refaced the cavern, grinning. "Let's get to it!"

52

ARON TOOK A swig of the thick drink that had been poured into his tankard. It carried a hard and bitter taste, and was nearly as dense as porridge. Planting it on the table, he turned his lips as he swallowed.

He couldn't believe people actually drank this stuff.

Lifting his head, he looked around the dim tavern that he now sat in.

It was a large community space in the town of Devon, with the town itself being a hotspot for traveling merchants due to its location between Bengai and Peluma. The room was filled with men and women, most of whom lived as farmers or other sorts of tradesmen based on their attire, and the scent of roasted meats, stew and alcohol hung heavily in the air. Laughter rang out from booths and small tables and somewhere in the corner, behind a group of people that Aaron couldn't see around, someone was playing a cithara.

There was a bar in the middle of the room, complete with cubbies of wine and small barrels of ale, and it was manned by a couple of bartenders who looked as rugged as any adventurer. A wrought-iron chandelier hung delicately from the ceiling, offering just a bit more light to the otherwise poorly sunlit room, and towards the back there was an ashy hearth beneath a stone mantlepiece. A group of middle-aged men were seated near it, their wiry hair tied into low ponytails or half-buns, and their bearded faces were split into delighted grins as they drank and ate merrily.

Aaron passed his slop of a drink a disgusted look.

"Anything I can get for ya?" A waiter came up to him, beer-bellied, a tattoo of a ship on his hairy arm, and a beard speckling his podgy cheeks. His graying hair was pulled into a low bun and over his unbelted tunic he wore a loose-fitting vest.

Aaron's bright blue eyes flashed at him. He didn't answer.

The man stared at him for a second, gathering his wits as Aaron lifted his mug and turned his drink idly. Even with his Avat ears covered by the loose hood of his cowl, he knew that the imperial recognized him.

Rubbing his mouth with a pudgy hand, the man threw a quick look across the crowded room. Then, he slammed his palms flat on the table and spoke to Aaron through clenched teeth. He kept his voice quiet. "How many times do you have to be told to not go wandering into the open like this without permission, boy?"

"What makes you think I don't have permission?" Aaron asked calmly.

The man didn't flinch. "You never have permission. One of these days, Aaron, your insatiable thirst for thrill is gonna get you lynched."

"I can handle myself, Thomas." Aaron forced down another gulp of his drink.

He wanted to throw up.

Figuring it wasn't worth it, he dumped it into the nearest potted plant when Thomas cast another anxious look around.

"What're you doing out here?" he continued, facing him again. "Here to cause unnecessary trouble? Hm? Get the chief to think I'm in cahoots with you and your always sneaking away? We haven't any auctions scheduled for another two weeks. You shouldn't be here."

"Two weeks?" Aaron gave him an honest look. "Didn't know that."

"How could you not? Aren't your intel scouts supposed to keep you all informed?"

"We haven't heard from them in a month."

The man faltered at that, his big, double-bagged eyes of gray searching Aaron's face for a joke.

Aaron's face was far from humored. "I left to find out why."

"On your own?"

"It's quicker that way."

"'It's quicker.'" Thomas grunted. "And how many days have you been out here, then?"

Aaron didn't meet his eyes, but he did release a soft sound of agitated discomfort.

Thomas huffed beneath his breath. "I thought so."

Aaron shifted and found his ground again. "We stationed Evan out here," he told the supporter. "He was one of the last scouts we'd heard from."

"Aye, Evan." Thomas nodded distractedly, recalling the name as well as the face that went with it.

He glanced over his shoulder. No one seemed to notice that he was spending so much time with this particular patron.

"He was here," he said quietly, circling back to Aaron. "But, same as you, I ain't seen him for days. Didn't think it'd already been a month since he'd last made contact with anyone."

"Well, it has been. People back home are worried. Aside from that auction update, is there anything else we should've heard about by now?"

Thomas' eyes flicked away and back before he leaned closer. "If you press me, I'd say word's going around that Empyrean's Guard has been growing increasingly suspicious of areas along the provincial border. Namely, Odelwhite."

Aaron scoffed. "They've always been suspicious, and our aetheriests handle it —"

"No, not like this, boy," Thomas interrupted with a shake of his head. "They may try to smoke you all out soon. You've all done well to get the general public to think that if you go too deep into Odelwhite you'll be harassed by ghosts and other apparitions. But some offhanded sightings of 'savages' running into that same forest shortly after news of a raid breaks have been causing the imperials to second-guess those stories."

"You think we have a rat?" Aaron discerned.

"Wouldn't be surprised. Not exactly safe, this business." Thomas straightened up. "May not be a supporter, but it could be a close friend trying to talk one *out* of their support, if you catch my drift."

"It's caught."

"There's one more thing."

"Don't keep me waiting."

"There's been talk of a certain…drink making its rounds across the Empire. Exclusive to Empyrean's Guard. People say it's rumored to give them unnatural abilities." He glanced up when someone chortled at a table and dropped his voice. "Abilities that students at the Aether Academy could only dream of having. I've heard most of this news coming from friends in Brusseir. Whatever it does, the guardsmen have been using it to crush Katruskik rebellions left and right. But, supposedly, those rebels are able to fight back."

"I heard something like that from a supporter over in Gilead," Aaron said. "But how're they fighting back if the Guards' new drug is making them so powerful?"

"Well, it —"

"Bartender!" a drunken man roared from afar, causing Thomas to jolt suddenly.

When he and Aaron looked over, the man was waving his tankard with a flushed face. He was surrounded by equally intoxicated friends.

"Refill!" he barked.

"Blasted idiots getting drunk at midday…" Thomas grumbled.

"You're the one serving alcohol at midday," Aaron pointed out plainly.

Thomas scowled at him.

"Bartender!"

"I'll be right with you!" Thomas shouted back and he picked up with Aaron where he'd left off. "Can't say I have an answer for you. Maybe the rebels are making their own drink to even the odds. Maybe they came across a supply of it somewhere. All I know, Aaron," Thomas gave him a dark look, "is that it doesn't look good. Doesn't sound good, either. Could very well have another continental war on our hands at this rate."

"Sounds dark."

"Bartender!"

"I'm comin'!" Thomas snapped.

"Maybe you should take care of that." Aaron nodded towards

the agitated guest. "Wouldn't wanna be the reason that your tavern gets poor reviews."

He smiled slyly and Thomas patted his shoulder with a low grumble. "I'll be seeing ya, boy. Stay out of trouble." He walked away.

As he departed, the distant clank of armor caught Aaron's ear.

Twisting in his chair, he peeked through the window beside him in time to spot a pair of soldiers marching across the tavern's threshold. A split second later the door popped open and the imperials marched in, their armor tinkling and pleated boots shuffling along.

Aaron readjusted himself in his seat. Then, he watched the soldiers out of the side of his eye.

They sat at a circular table near the bar. From there they were still in Aaron's line of sight — and he in theirs — and after learning what the men would like to drink a waiter stepped away from them.

Aaron closed his eyes.

He was no full-blooded Avat, but his mother had taught him how to discern the different sounds around him well enough. Frowning through the absent-minded babbling, the chortling, the crude jokes and the aside comments, he soon found himself homing in on the soldiers' voices.

"...seems like this place is calm enough," one of them was saying to the other. "I'd kill for something to happen, though, these slow days are always the worst."

"Least we got to supervise that auction the other day." His partner nodded a quick thanks when one of the waitresses brought their drinks over. "I'm still not surprised that that last she-devil went for as much as it did. It's well-built, if you know what I mean." He waggled his eyebrows and his friend laughed.

Aaron scoffed quietly, but tucked the man's information in mind.

As Thomas had said, there were still auctions going on.

He wondered how many Taranis had managed to miss in the last month.

"Looks like the old man finally fixed this place up a bit," the other one remarked, looking around the tavern. "Still doesn't feel too far off from that backwater hideout me and William raided over in Ribbosheth. Wouldn't be surprised if there were devils hiding beneath the floorboards."

"Hmph, it'd give us something to do at least," his partner grunted, grabbing his drink.

The other soldier laughed. "By the way, I heard Viceroy Diomedes finally issued a statement about that Skylok last week. Said there's no connection between him and the goblin at all."

His partner snorted as he took a swig of his order. "Like that'll stop the rumors. I've got a friend in the slave trading business who saw Skylok himself and swears it looks just like the viceroy."

"Hm." His friend swirled his mug thoughtfully. "Odd."

Aaron was intrigued by that. But when the men's conversation drifted into talks of getting their armor refitted, he had to seek out other tidbits of intel.

Searching the room still with his ears, he soon found himself dropping in on a different group just a stone's throw away from him. Their voices were lower, as if they were discussing some deep secret, and so Aaron had to strain himself just a little in order to overhear.

"…Yeah, I mean, I dunno if it's true," a young man was saying to the small group that was seated with him. "The town's practically been cut off from outside travelers since it happened, and there's a blockade of soldiers over a mile out so you can't even get close to the place. But I'd say that's evidence enough."

"Wow…Orinn, huh?" one of his friends asked, unwittingly sharing the topic of their conversation with Aaron's unwelcome ears. "And it's burnt to the ground?"

With his head still ducked low and his body still, Aaron's eyes snapped open. Lifting them, he pinpointed the gossips.

The strangers were seated near a foggy window and looked to be only a few years older than he. Plates of food that were nearly scraped clean were resting in front of them, and empty glasses that were still stained with froth were near them. Clearly their meal was over, allowing them to level their full attention to the talk that they were engaged in.

Shifting his eyes so that he wouldn't be caught staring — although with how crowded the room was there was little chance anyone would've noticed — Aaron continued to listen.

"I heard it was just Lord Elkiah's mansion that got destroyed," the first townsman continued. "The earl. And I heard that people as far away as Inglave could hear this creepy howling coming from Orinn on the same night of the attack. Said it sounded like a pack of monsters."

"That's freaky," another one of his companions remarked.

"You're tellin' me." The first man tossed a quick look at the room and dropped his voice a bit more. "People think the attack… was led by *Saruke's Shade.*"

There was an oddly dramatic pause.

Aaron didn't move. He just waited.

Finally, one of the men snorted. "That's just an urban legend."

"C'mon, even you can't still be a skeptic!" his friend retorted. "Stories about Saruke's Shade have been circling Nassaul for the past year. The bigwigs and politicians want you to think he's fake, so it doesn't cause a panic. But my uncle does business in Nassaul, and from what he's said I can tell you that the Shade is no legend. People wish the Empire'd do something about him but for now, they're willing to turn a blind eye, or cover up his acts with scapegoats and made-up stories to make the people think it's not that bad.

"But what I think…" the man leaned back with a small smile, "is that Saruke's Shade is an omen. A harbinger. You know how things've been getting out of hand lately, what with the Katruskik Alliance, and rumors of war, and those goblins and their hired savages attacking the slave trade, upending the economy. Empyrean and Vedrah are angry with us, I bet. Mad that we Arkanians can't keep this blasted hole running smoothly."

"What're we s'posed to even do to appease them?" another countered in exasperation. "The emperor's already called for an increase in sacrifices. My family is poor, we can barely keep up! It's like as soon as we buy a slave, we have to surrender it as a sacrifice and buy another!"

"I guess Saruke's Shade'll have to visit you, then."

"You're a real git, you know that?"

The friend cackled.

"Why do they even call him that, anyway?" another one asked.

"Saruke's Shade. What's that even mean?"

"Dunno." The man who'd told the tale shrugged a shoulder. "All I know is that they say he's dressed in black, with a mask that could make the blood of an axe-murderer run cold…"

Aaron removed himself from their conversation, and the hubbub of the tavern rose around him.

Saruke's Shade…he'd never heard of that name. Not even any of the intelligence scouts had mentioned it before they'd disappeared. He wondered if it was because news of it was finally beginning to break in Lyrik, or if it was due to something else.

Either way, the word "Saruke" carried a certain familiarity to it.

He racked his brain for the answer. Where could he have possibly heard it before?

His eyes lit up when it hit him.

"Hey." A close voice cut through his thoughts like a dagger.

He tilted his gaze.

An older man was standing next to his table. Just over his shoulder, Aaron could see that he'd brought a few friends along with him.

At first glance they seemed to be normal men of the town. But a second look proved that they were more likely to be from beyond Devon's borders: their leather breastplates and padded shoulders suggested battle expertise, while their swords, daggers — and in one's case a tomahawk — implied that those battles were likely unprompted and trifling. So far as Aaron knew, Devon wasn't the sort of place that would birth such thuggish characters.

"I have question for you, boy," the one at the front said. He was tall and big-shouldered, and his hardened arms were uncovered. Leather gauntlets encased his forearms, and he wore an entelodon-skin loincloth over a pair of thick, rustic trousers. The sides of his head were shaved, leaving him to pull the long locks that were on his crown into a neck-length braid, and his beard was brutal-looking, but full.

Aaron immediately noticed his accent.

He was Katruskik.

"What's your question?" he asked.

"You look familiar." The sides of the man's blue eyes twitched. "Maybe you owe me money."

Aaron couldn't help but bark out a laugh that he was sure the man didn't appreciate.

He couldn't help it. The encounter was far too cliché for him to have reacted any other way.

"Ya uyatisch, shto ne tiots astazavs s tohrep-ayanpulazdop," he said, the Katruskan words flowing over his tongue like water.

I make it a point to not get involved with peehole-dandruff.

The man's eyes bulged at him.

Aaron wanted to laugh again. He really did.

But he kept a straight face.

"Ot Katruskik?" the man asked, his face one of fierce intensity as he demanded Aaron's ethnic heritage. The fact that the two possibly had something in common didn't seem to be thrilling for him.

Holding his gaze, Aaron stood up. "Yeah."

The man stared at him for a moment, his lip curling in horror and disgust. He studied Aaron's features.

Finally, he chuckled. Then, laughing outright, he backhanded the arm of one of his posse. *"Uhn kivorkulop!"* He laughed in Aaron's face, amused and condescending of the raider's mixed heritage, which he'd so proudly pointed out.

As if Aaron didn't know of it himself.

The man's friends joined in his laughter.

Deadpan, Aaron waited for them to finish.

When they quieted, he looked at their leader. His icy blue eyes were daggers. *"Ot taarenehged."*

Lightning snapped through the man's eyes and in a flash he seized Aaron by the collar, nearly hauling him off of his feet. Slamming him against the wall, he held him there.

At the surrounding tables, people stopped talking and looked up.

Aaron wasn't entirely surprised by the man's reaction. He wouldn't have liked to have been called a degenerate either.

Just out of the side of his eye, he spotted Thomas at the bar. He was staring at the escalating encounter, bug-eyed.

"Ot yonshems, osh-il?" the man growled into Aaron's face, his mother-tongue thick with indignation.

Aaron didn't stop himself. "Not as funny as your breath."

The man sneered and for a second Aaron expected him to physically lash out. He tensed readily, his arm flinching.

But instead the man's eyes carefully shifted away from Aaron's face and landed on something outside. When he looked at the raider again, slowly this time, his fury subsided just enough to give way to a cunning grin.

Aaron's eyes tightened.

What was he thinking?

"All right, that's enough, break it up!" Thomas barged into the gathering and separated the man from Aaron. Holding the half-Avat back with one hand, he stood flat-footed before the strangers. "I'll not be having a brawl in my pub, thank you very much. If you need to fight, go to the town's notice board, see if anyone needs a group of muscle-heads to hunt down some pesky beast."

The bearded man smiled, his teeth winking brilliantly. Then, he spat at Thomas' feet.

Thomas drew his toe back with a dark look.

"We will finish outside," the man said. His eyes were on Aaron. "Or will you hide behind fat bartender, like little boy?"

Aaron's features sharpened, likening his face unto that of a hunting wildcat.

Thomas spiraled to see him, but as soon as he saw Aaron's expression he knew it was too late.

He tried anyway. "Don't," he said quietly. "You know you shouldn't be out here. Don't make this worse for yourself."

Aaron glared at him.

Then with one arm, he moved the man out of his way and stepped forward.

He held the Katruskik warrior's gaze with a challenging stare of his own. "Outside."

53

UPON HEARING AARON'S acceptance of the challenge, Thomas closed his eyes and sighed.

The Katruskik man smiled approvingly and dropped a hand onto his sword as he headed for the door. His men followed him.

So did Aaron.

Thomas watched them go helplessly.

If there was anything he'd learned about Chief Ivan's son, it was that once he'd put his mind to something there was no convincing him otherwise.

Around him, the patrons who'd noticed the altercation followed the group with their eyes, and they leaned and craned and peeked to see what they were about to do.

The soldiers also glanced up before exchanging looks.

The main square of Devon was just outside of the tavern. Normally filled with the carriages and mule-led carts of merchants that were passing through, it was mostly empty. Only a handful of craftsmen and other salesmen were manning stands along the edges of the plaza, bargaining with the villagers that had come to see them or selling their wares at fixed prices. Not once did any of them pass Aaron or the men who were with him a second glance.

The group circled to the side of the tavern, and followed the short road there to a dead-end.

There, the group leader turned to Aaron and drew his broadsword. It was a thick blade, straight, with a padded grip and a cross-guard that was edged with animal fur.

He spun it absently, still wearing that same crafty look from earlier.

Aaron came to a stop in front of him. No sooner had he done so did he notice that the man's allies were forming a circle around him. Their hands were already on their weapons.

Keeping his eyes trained on them, Aaron lifted a gloved hand and grabbed his tonfa. They were belted to the back of his waist, out of sight.

"Normally, I do not fight children. But…" The leader bobbed his sword at Aaron indicatively. "You are different."

"Funny, I was about to say the same thing." Aaron didn't fight a smile this time. It was a chilling one, and showed no humor.

He got a short, bitter laugh as a response. "Is funny. You goblins like to act tough. But then run when things get too hot."

Aaron tensed. He tried to counter. "A goblin, am I?"

"You are Blaze." The man pointed his sword at him again, smiling darkly, and then he gestured to the others with it. "And we…are bounty hunters."

Slowly, Aaron's smile fell away.

"Your poster is on pole outside tavern. And everywhere else." The leader was smug, clearly aware that he had the upper hand in that moment. "This is when I knew." He tapped his temple. "You see? I do not forget faces."

Aaron's jaw shifted, but he said nothing.

So that's what had distracted him after he'd pinned Aaron to the wall. He'd glanced outside and spotted one of his wanted posters.

Aaron stared at him for a space of time, bewildered by his own carelessness. At last his lips curled upward, and a diamond gleam entered his eye.

He could act like they'd made a mistake. Shrug off the accusation and beat them senseless if they tried to press the matter.

But where'd be the fun in that?

"Well…" Slowly, he unholstered his tonfa. Spinning them against his forearms, he dropped his hips into a battle stance. "Looks like you found me."

At that, the face of the Katruskik warrior morphed into hardened preparation. Bending at the knee, he readied his blade.

His men likewise readied themselves, drawing their weapons, dropping into stances.

Aaron looked around at them, analyzing their poses, discerning their skill, their abilities.

He wasn't the least bit scared.

He'd been in the Empire for a week, forced to rein in his anger every time he encountered masters with their Avat slaves, or heard the imperials speaking of them as if they had less value than livestock. At almost every turn he'd been reminded that their bodies were viewed as property, they were whipped like cattle, they were chained in storefront windows, slaughtered as sacrifices, beaten and sold like trinkets…and for what?

Arkanian pride. The imperials even turned that same disdain onto their own countrymen if they dared to stand up for the Avats. It made him ill.

So he'd been itching to blow off steam for a while now.

"Well?" he looked between them.

If one thing was true it was that his title, Blaze, described his fighting style just as accurately as it did his hotheadedness. But he didn't care for that. All he knew was that he hadn't clobbered an imperial in the name of freedom in close to a month. Now that the opportunity had presented itself, and with his own freedom on the line at that, the desire to expend the energy that had been building up in his bones was blinding.

"Don't keep me waiting!" he shouted. "I thought you wanted my bounty! What, you waiting for me to faint with fear so you can drag me away?"

Movement behind him.

Something heavy spun though the air.

Aaron whirled about, his guard already up, and he sidestepped the tomahawk that sought to cleave his head.

In an instant the hunter who'd thrown it was upon him — machete bared, eyes wide, mouth open.

Deflecting his attacks, Aaron front-kicked him in the face, making him stagger.

Another hunter fell on him with a pair of daggers and lashed out with gutless precision.

Dodging the first few blows with twinkling steps, Aaron barred his tonfa in front of his face and blocked left, right, ducked, then spun away when one of the man's knives came swooping down for his face.

The blade caught the nape of his cloak instead, and as Aaron twisted out of reach it was torn off of him.

Though dressed in imperial wear that consisted of leather belts, a tunic, padded leg guards and dark trousers, without his cloak his messy red hair and pointy ears made the entire outfit fall apart.

Clicking his tongue, he smashed the button in the sides of his handlebars.

Immediately, his tonfa blades popped out. They blinked wildly when he spun them against his forearms.

Raising his guard he glanced around at the bounty hunters, calculating their next moves, who'd come first, how many.

So much for taking it easy.

"Get him!" the leader yelled.

Two of them came at him this time: the one with the daggers and another who was armed with a double-headed war hammer complete with a spike.

The one with the daggers closed in first, swiping at Aaron with whipping blows that he either deflected or dodged outright. The one with the hammer acted as backup, swinging his weapon with a scream whenever there was an opening. He was much slower than his ally but based on the rush of wind that Aaron felt whenever he avoided him, he knew that what the man lacked in speed he certainly made up for in strength.

Adrenaline pounded through his veins, sharpened all of his senses. His eyes brightened.

Dispatching the hunter's daggers in what almost looked like a dance, he flung them at the man with the hammer. Once, twice he struck him in the stomach and then, grappling him, he hurled him into his ally.

They crashed into a stack of crates.

The man with the hammer recovered first. He swung at Aaron's ribs and missed, and ended up suffering a broken arm and nose before getting kicked into the back of a stone house.

He crashed into it with a sickening *crack* and slid to the ground.

The hunter with a machete ran in next, and he held his ground against the raider for all of a few seconds. Soon he was disarmed, and when Aaron all but broke his shins he dropped face-first onto his ally's hammer.

Whirling his tonfa Aaron faced the leader, who braced himself.

He sneered. "Scared yet?"

With little more than a snarl, the leader charged.

It seemed that a surge of adrenaline was racing through his veins as well, for he moved with a certain speed and skill that his flunkies had lacked. Reworking his own strategy Aaron launched a straight jab that, to his surprise, the hunter ducked beneath.

Dipping his shoulder, he rammed it into Aaron's gut and sent him stumbling backward.

Aaron gasped, nearly winded, and he lifted his guard right as the hunter rushed him once more.

For a time they were evenly matched, catching attacks on their blades, landing kicks, throwing elbows. The air rang with the peal of metal crashing against metal, of shuffling feet, of the heavy *thumps* of connecting blows; dust kicked up around their feet.

At last, Aaron changed stances and whirled his tonfa like windmills, overwhelming his opponent with a bladed tornado of seamless strikes and rapid-fire kicks that backed him into a corner.

Aaron didn't let up: switching it up again he jabbed his tonfa blades into the hunter's side — but was blocked.

Turning on the heel of his foot, Aaron swung his arms in a downward arc that brought his blades crashing onto the man's cross-guard, knocking the sword out of his hand.

Pivoting, he slammed his heel into the hunter's neck.

The man winced, clearly impaired. But he wobbled defiantly and took a couple of steps towards the young raider.

Aaron waited for a second, tonfa up.

When the imperial showed no sign of succumbing, he kicked him in the side of the head.

The hunter was out cold before he'd even hit the ground.*tv*

OUTLAWS
CODE: BOUNTY

"Hey!"

Aaron turned.

The soldiers from the tavern were jogging down the street towards him.

"Is that —?" One of them stopped.

"It *is* Blaze!" the other one gaped.

"You mean it took out all those guys on its own?"

His partner cursed and drew his sword. "Blasted monster..."

Battered and stained with blood that mostly wasn't his, Aaron raised his tonfa.

"Aaron!" a voice hissed.

His eyes flicked to the side.

Thomas was standing at the end of a narrow alley just to his right.

"This way!" he whispered, waving at him.

Aaron glanced from him to the soldiers and back.

It didn't take long for the imperials to figure out what he was thinking.

"Stop right there!" one of them yelled, running to him.

Lowering his tonfa, Aaron reached into one of the pouches that were belted to his side and lobbed something at them. Then he hopped into the alley after Thomas, who hastily led him away.

Behind them, the grenade Aaron had tossed detonated with a roar.

The buildings shook, the ground jumped. Smoke billowed into the alleyway after them.

People started screaming.

The soldiers started shouting.

"Where'd it go?!"

"Check the alley!"

"In here." Thomas brought Aaron to the back of the tavern and lifted a cellar door that was near the rear entrance.

Spinning his tonfa so that their blades would retract, Aaron shoved them back into their holsters and jumped into the hole.

"And take this." Thomas dropped a bandana in after him, which Aaron caught. "Town's gonna be on lockdown now that you've been spotted. This'll take you right out. You'll end up at an old supporter's place — head west, it'll bring you out to the royal highway. Keep going, and you'll reach Odelwhite by at least midday tomorrow, on foot. Keep your head down, Aaron," he added warningly.

"Same to you," Aaron said. "Don't get caught."

Thomas smirked. "I've been through worse, boy."

Voices and shouting came from the other end of the alley.

The soldiers were coming.

"Go!" Thomas urged, and he slammed the door.

Aaron heard it bolt shut.

Feeling his way through the darkness, he soon found the rugged, earthy frame of a tunnel. He plunged into it.

The roar of voices and the screaming of startled townsfolk carefully died away as he maneuvered his way through the passage, eventually leaving him to venture through the blackness in silence.

At long last he felt the ground creep upward and he caught himself before he could trip up a set of earthen stairs. Climbing to their peak, he stretched his hands out and touched what felt like the sanded face of another set of doors.

He pushed against them.

They barely budged.

He tried again.

They leaped an inch.

With a growl, he shoved them.

This time they flew open, and what sounded like a heavy beam of wood tumbled away. It had likely been the reason for the doors being jammed.

Panting quietly, Aaron crawled out of the tunnel and gripped the doorframe to hoist himself above ground. Stepping into the open, he looked around to determine his new location.

He was in a wide open plain, with lumping hills and jagged mountains ringing the distant skyline in the east, while a dark road at the other end of a field of waist-high grass wound back towards Devon.

He glanced around, curious as to where the supposed home of the supporter that Thomas had mentioned could possibly be.

He stepped forward and jerked to a stop when his foot crushed something. Surprise lifted his eyebrows.

He *was* in the supporter's home.

But it was nothing more than a heaping pile of ash and rubble.

A cold wind blew past, causing a rusted bucket to roll across what had once been a polished wooden floor. It was stopped by a mat of overgrown weeds, which had spread to infest most of what remained of the house's ground level.

Lifting his eyes, Aaron studied what was left of the home.

From the looks of it, it had been destroyed by a fire. The roof was gone and the framework had been reduced to a mere skeleton of its former self. Only a few walls were still left intact, and trails of inky soot marred the sills of the remaining windows.

At the sound of an eerie creaking, Aaron spun on the spot.

There was a door hanging off of its rusty hinges. The wind had just caused it to shift a bit.

He calmed himself and took another look around.

The fire had been arson, that much was for certain, and it had been controlled: there was no sign of damage anywhere else in the field. The burnt property was just an ugly scar in the middle of boundless nature.

His sharp eyes fell across the ruins again, and they narrowed at the sight of a strange, gray-and-black powder that was sprinkled all over the ground.

His heart sank with understanding.

Tossing his eyes up and around, he searched for the evidence of what he already trusted to be true. It didn't take him very long to locate it.

It was a sign, hammered into what had once been the front yard.

Going to it, he circled to its front.

Its words were painted in the curvy lettering of the Arkanian alphabet and were scripted from right to left. Since it wasn't a letter it was to be read one line across at a time, rather than down, and as Aaron read its message his stomach sank still further:

Lecil Family

On Suspicion of Keeping Goblins from the Empire
This Property has been Confiscated By Imperial Law

Upheld by the Empire's Loyal Tradesmen of Able Servants
In the 12th Year of His Imperial Majesty,
Emperor Koberius Arkania

Aaron stepped back and looked the home over again. Or, what was left of it.

This supporter's home had been burnt to the ground just over three years ago.

Right…that was what happened to those who dared to offer their homes as a sanctuary to runaway slaves. Their homes were destroyed, and then they themselves were sold into slavery. Sometimes even their family members were forced to suffer the same fate, if the Empire could uncover even a hint of their cooperation.

It seemed that whoever this family had been, they'd been dealt that fateful hand.

Guilt pinched at his insides.

It didn't last for very long. He soon reminded himself that the supporters knew the risks of defying the imperial slave trade. They always did.

He only wished those risks weren't so cruel.

54

LEAVING HARVER'S BELONGINGS behind, Brent and the others followed the incline that descended from the cliff and ventured deeper into the cavern. There they split up, with each group heading to their predetermined location. Upon arriving, they took to their assignments.

Removing their weapons, slippers and extra sashes, Brent and Mekial got ready to dive for Harver's shells.

In the slightly forested area on the other side of the cave, Eklaire, Liam and Renée split up to hunt for the rubbershrooms.

"Geronimo!" Mekial cried, tucking his knees into his chest, and he cannonball'd into the lake.

"Just grab enough lake shells to fill this bag," Harver said to Brent as Mekial resurfaced and paddled in gleeful circles. She held up the sack that she was speaking of: it was a drawstring bag that looked capable of carrying at least a few pounds' worth of materials.

"Got it." Taking the pouch Brent started for the lake, only to stop and look back at her. "You're not coming in?"

"Of course not!" Harver frowned. "There's a bit of tinkering I need to do with some stuff from my bag —"

" — You mean your house? — "

"— it's not my house! So I won't be coming in. Not just yet at least. After I'm done, I'll have to search another area near here for something else."

Brent shrugged. "Suit yourself. But you're gonna miss out!"

Tossing the bag by the lakeside he plugged his nose and jumped in, creating such a great splash that Harver was caught in it.

With her dark bangs spilling into her eyes, she shook off her damp arms. "Ugh…Brent!"

He popped out of the water, laughing.

"Ugh…" Pulling a tasseled rag out of her satchel, Harver proceeded to dry her face off as Brent swam away.

"The water's so warm!" Mekial exclaimed, treading water a short distance from him.

"That's probably because the sun's hitting it," Brent reckoned. An idea struck him. "Hey, wanna see who can gather twenty shells first?"

"You're on!" the boy exclaimed.

"On three! One, two…!"

Taking a breath, they dove out of sight.

The world reverted to a realm of soft blues and twinkling lights as soon as they opened their eyes below. The lake's true shape was also made known to them, showing itself to be a descending, cylindrical tunnel rather than bowl-shaped, like the lake in the valley. It was also brighter, what with the sunlight, allowing even the lake's coral-encrusted bottom to be visible. Schools of freshwater fish drifted around the hard-bodied lifeforms, ranging from exotic cross-species to blue angelfish and guppies.

Mekial delightedly swam through them.

Brent fixed his eyes elsewhere.

Coral was growing out of parts of the craggy walls, and surrounding them were all manner of lake shells. Varying in size and shape, they were embedded into the walls like decorum, while larger ones were scattered at the bottom.

Brent and Mekial looked at one another. Then, they stroked their way towards the walls and began their excavation.

Mekial set his eyes on a rather large shell first. It was so big that even pulling on it with both hands couldn't make it budge.

But he kept yanking anyway, his face scrunching up.

Already carrying an armful of his own small shells, Brent noticed. Abandoning his findings, he swam towards the boy and tried to offer his help.

Together, the two pulled the shell free — and unleashed a storm of bubbles along with it.

Mekial opened his mouth as if to let out a cry of triumph, but all that came out were more bubbles. Clutching his treasure, he pedaled for the surface.

Brent loitered behind and peered into the hole that had been revealed upon their success. It was wide enough for his arm to fit through, and it was rimmed with all kinds of shells and precious stones that he knew the village craftsmen preferred.

He smiled to himself.

Up above, Mekial emerged from the lake with a noisy gasp. "Harver!" he cried. "Look what I found!"

Caught in the middle of twisting a screwdriver into a tiny, unidentified gadget, Harver looked up at him.

Mekial swam closer and pulled his great shell out of the water for her to see. "One giant lake shell!"

Harver's eyes grew, reflecting the light that bounced off of the discovery. "Ooh…"

"Neat, huh?" Mekial grinned.

"Yeah." Harver took it. It weighed less than it looked and it was as big as a vanity mirror. She could even see her reflection in it. "Wait, how'm I s'posed to fit this in my bag…?"

"That totally has to count as twenty," Mekial claimed and he backstroked proudly. "I bet Brent's just gonna come up with a little handful of teeny-weeny lake shells!" He snickered. "I win!"

Thump.

Harver and Mekial followed the sound.

Brent had just returned and had dumped his recovery onto the shore: a heaping pile of shells and glittering stones.

Even Harver was impressed.

"Where did you find these?!" Mekial snatched up a shiny rock that flashed all kinds of yellows when he held it up to the sun. "Is this calcinite?! Better make sure Heldar knows about it…"

"Sometimes it pays to dig around a little more," Brent claimed, puffed up by their amazement. "I think I win this round."

"Well, you did find pretty rocks…whoa, Harver, look at this one!" Snatching up a stone that glittered like a multi-colored galaxy,

Mekial showed it to her.

Harver took it and examined it closely. What she said next had little to do with it. "Y'know, you've always been good at holding your breath underwater, Brent." She eyed him suspiciously. "You're like a fish."

"Who, me?" He avoided her gaze. "I just, uh, had lots of practice."

"Practice holding your breath?"

"Yup." Brent wiped a bit more water off of his face.

"Huh." Harver went back to examining the rock.

"Don't even think I know what these look like," Liam confessed, parting the leaves of a low-lying bush on the other side of the cavern. He squinted around for a second. "What even is a 'rubbershroom'?"

"I think Harver was trying to say that it's a mushroom with a weird texture…" Renée replied distractedly and she knelt to press her face towards a patch of grass. A black and white butterfly that had been resting there flew away hurriedly. "Wonder how big they are…"

Movement flashed in the upper corner of her eye.

Leaning back she looked up, and she watched as a medium-sized bird soared though one of the holes in the ceiling and landed on one of the cliffs above her.

It was a slender fowl with smooth, silver and white feathers, a long, arching neck, tall legs and an orange, boat-billed mouth. Its most telling feature however, were the dark feathers on its head, which flowed out of its skull in a way that resembled hair.

Eklaire saw it, too and she gasped. "Look, ya'll! It's a proardea!"

"Where?" Liam asked, looking up. Squinting in the sunlight, he shaded his eyes.

"Up there!" Renée pointed.

The bird, one that they knew was familiar to the plains surrounding Taranis, tilted its head and noticed their attention. Spreading its wings as if in show, it released a low, honking quack — a sound that, strangely enough, wasn't unlike that of an angry brass instrument.

"Ugh, who farted?!" they heard Mekial shout from the lake.

"Don't look at me!" Harver returned.

"There are bubbles behind Brent! Was it you?!"

"Those're fish!" Brent countered. "It was probably you! He who knew it, blew it!"

"And he who protested it, foam-crested it!"

"He who quipped it, ripped it!"

"He who rued it, brewed it!"

"Should I tell them?" Renée wondered aloud as the boys' creative dispute continued.

"I wouldn't," Liam said.

Ignorant of their interaction, the proardea waddled forward and dug its beak into a bush, freeing a clump of leaves and what looked like a cluster of dark berries. Smacking its beak as it devoured the small snack, it spread its wings and took off with another quack.

"Whoa!"

At the sound of Eklaire's voice, Liam and Renée looked at her. She was crouching in front of a pair of closely-set rocks, hands on her knees.

"Did you find the rubbershroom?" Renée asked.

"Nope!" Eklaire said. "But I think I just found a new creature!"

Liam and Renée looked at one another before approaching, but right as Liam knelt to see what had their friend so enthralled, Renée spotted a peculiar object elsewhere and went to investigate.

Paying no mind to her, Liam and Eklaire leaned closer to the crevice that was formed by the rocks' proximity. Inside there was a large, wide-antlered beetle whose entire body, save its head, was fluctuating a fiery orange.

Its back shuddered, revealing a pair of wings that flashed into being before hiding away again, and it turned its horned head from the villagers as if it was embarrassed.

Eklaire wrinkled her nose. "It's kinda ugly."

Suddenly the beetle revealed its wings, and with a low buzz it zipped into Eklaire's face.

Shrieking, she tried swatting it away with her arms.

It seemed to dodge her effortlessly, but was eventually caught by her forearm.

She wailed. "Eww, I touched it!"

Buzzing noisily, the insect flew into her face again and gave her nose a little jolt.

She yelped and grabbed her face.

The beetle took off.

Liam watched it go. "Maybe you shouldn't have bugged it."

"Oh, hardy-har-har!" Eklaire turned on him, still plugging her nose. Her voice sounded nasally.

Liam looked at her, his poker-face steadfast. After a short second it broke, and he turned away with a snicker.

Eklaire frowned. "What're you laughin' at?! That critter nearly zapped my nose off!"

Liam kept sniggering.

"I found it!" Renée exclaimed, causing the two to look up and find her.

She was standing atop a rock that hugged a large boulder right beside them. Leaning against it with one hand, she was holding her found item in the other triumphantly.

Although it wasn't identical to any kind of mushroom that they'd ever seen, there were some ways in which it showed that Harver's description of it had been remotely accurate. For instance, its thick stem was mushroom-like but stockier, and it had an interesting texture that certainly made it look rubbery.

But what they found to be the most intriguing was that it was a richly saturated blue, to the point that it almost seemed to glow.

"At least, I think I found it…" Renée, having also acknowledged the mushroom's color, lowered it in discouragement. After a moment of thought, she clenched it resolutely and took a deep breath. *"Harver!"* she hollered, looking up, and her voice thundered around them. *"The rubbershrooms are blue, right?!"*

Liam cringed. His ears were ringing.

Eklaire noticed and worriedly looked from him to Renée.

"They're blue!" came Harver's distant and nearly imperceptible reply.

"How many?!"

"Get twelve!"

"'Kay!" Renée's eyes dropped to Liam.

He was unhappily twisting a pinky into his ear.

"Oops." She smiled weakly, clutching the rubbershroom to her chest. "Sorry!"

Twelve rubbershrooms and a large pile of lake shells later, they were done.

After meeting at the site of their arrival, Renée, Eklaire and Liam added their rubbershrooms to the shells that Brent and Mekial had gathered.

Once Harver had tied the bag shut Liam offered to carry it, mentioning that by now they would need to divide the baggage amongst one another anyway.

Though embarrassed that she had to accept help, Harver consented and gave the sack to him.

At the same time, Brent picked up her hefty backpack and swung it over his shoulder. He made it look light.

"And did you find anything that's already compatible with the storehouse that you brought along with you?" he asked knowingly.

Harver pressed her lips taut and avoided his eyes. "No…"

"Aw, cheer up, Harv!" Eklaire patted her back. "I'm sure you'll find more stuff next time. Hate to say I toldja so, though."

Harver groaned. "No you don't…"

Eklaire giggled.

Filing out of the cavern, they ventured back into the network of caves that made up Heletia. Partway through it Harver secured her candle-hat once more and lit it with her nail guards. The flame jumped to life a couple of tunnels away from what Mekial recalled to be the luka's chamber.

He glanced around the gloomy cave when they stepped into it, a hand on one of his knives.

The first thing he noticed was that, unlike when they'd first come in, he couldn't spot a pair of glowing green eyes watching them from anywhere. Had the creature gone elsewhere?

Ahead of him, Liam attuned all of his senses to his hearing, for his eyesight did little for him, even in the candlelight.

A split second later he heard a distant rustle of movement followed by the clatter of pebbles dropping to the ground. But it was all so soft that, were he not an Avat with albinism, he surely would've missed it.

Fortunately, that wasn't the case. "Stay sharp," he said. "Luka's still here."

"Okay," Eklaire consented, staying close to the group.

Mekial gulped.

Renée studied the cave tensely, a hand on her sword.

Towards the middle of the group, Harver shivered when a draft whispered across her shoulders. All at once, she sneezed.

Her head swung forward violently and her candle-hat went fly-ing. With a sharp crash the glass casing broke apart and the candle rolled away, where it was extinguished in a small puddle of water.

Harver sniffed. "Oops."

The raiders steeled themselves.

Liam looked around, for a new and excited scuffle of motion had reached him: the scraping of claws and the hollow flap of thick, folded wings bending as they moved.

"Huddle," he said sharply.

As one, the entire group huddled together in the middle of the darkness, with Liam, Brent and Renée on the outer ring while Eklaire, Harver and Mekial were trapped in their circle.

Mekial felt his throat go dry.

"It's coming," Liam said quietly, more so to Brent than anyone else.

"Yeah," he whispered back. "I can hear it."

"Do you have another candle, Harver?" Renée asked urgently, drawing her sword.

"Uh, i-in my bag," the girl stammered.

"Get it." Brent lowered Harver's bag off of his shoulder, but he didn't turn from the cave.

Harver rustled through it for a second, and her skin prickled. Glancing up, she let loose a piteous squeak.

A pair of bright green eyes had just rounded a pillar and were carefully drifting towards them, their pupils stretched into tall slits.

Brent was the only one facing them directly. Reaching back, he gripped one of his bladed staffs.

At the same time the luka's large, slitted eyes dragged a distant memory to the forefront of his mind: flaming passages, billowing smoke, a pressing weight —

— A malformed eye of gold, whose slit pupil was brightened by a red mark that hung within it —

The recollection was choppy. But it was there.

Always there, taunting him from the shadows of his past.

The luka hissed dangerously. Thanks to the darkness its entire body was hard to make out, but they could identify the furry outline of its mantled silhouette as well as the folds of its large, webbed wings. Their clawed tips scratched the ground as it crawled close and when it parted its fangs, they caught a draft of its molding meat-breath.

Eklaire gagged.

Renée fought the urge to do the same.

"Okay…" Brent kept his voice quiet. "No one make…any… sudden…mo —"

Mekial, who'd been panting fearfully, yelled wildly and rushed at the beast, one knife raised to attack.

"Mekial!" Renée yelled.

"Stop —!" Brent reached out to grab him but missed.

Growling like a rabid dog, the luka lunged to snatch the boy's head off.

In that same instant its fiendish cry reverberated, bounced, landed in Liam's ears and gave him full command of the cavern's size — along with the luka's exact location.

Slinging something out of his waist sash, he hurled it at the monster.

The spinning object was shaped like a gear, with several bulbs sticking out of it like spurs. It smacked the luka in the side of its face, and on impact purple gas spewed out of its protrusions.

The animal screeched — a high-pitched, chittering, staccato sound that made Brent, Liam and Harver stagger and grab their ears.

"Block your eyes!" Brent yelled, and with his free hand he reached into his waist sash and threw something at the ground.

It erupted on contact, creating a blinding flicker of strobe lights that made the luka reel away in agony.

Renée grabbed Mekial right before it could crash into him.

"C'mon! Move!" Brent ordered, urging the others out of the

cave, and as they took off he snatched up Harver's backpack and ran after them.

The luka chitter-screeched again, its eyes red from the smoke-bomb Liam had thrown, and it galumphed after them in a rage.

"Go, go, go!" Brent yelled as they entered the next cave.

Roaring the luka tore after them, batting aside stalagmites and kicking loose boulders out of its way.

"Stay ahead of me!" Renée shouted, ushering Eklaire, Harver and Mekial along, and she rounded on the luka. Grabbing something from her sash, she bit off a wire that was attached to it and threw it with all her might.

The little sphere exploded with a *pop-bang!* over the beast's head and it staggered in surprise. Stumbling, it crashed into a pillar with a dastardly moan.

"Good work," Brent praised, and the two of them rushed to catch up with everyone.

The luka reoriented itself with a shake of its head. Howling, it tore after them again, lumbering, growling, galloping in a way that was so diabolical it was as if it'd bounded right out of a nightmare.

Eyes ahead, the villagers jumped into the next cave, where sunlight finally broke through the gloom to embrace them. Together they weaved between the narrow aisle of stalagmites, scrambling out of the dark to enter the light. Eklaire nearly tripped, only to catch her footing when Liam grabbed her by the arm. Renée seized Mekial's.

Gasping, they stumbled into the day and looked back in time to see the luka recoil at the edge of the light. Without the darkness to cloak it they could see that it was quite large, towering at least two feet over Liam, with a hairless, gray head and matching claws that turned black at the ends. Its tunneled nostrils flared and as it winked its green eyes shut it swung away from the sun, chittering horribly.

The Avats of the party winced, but since the sound could no longer echo around them, they weren't as disoriented. Together with the others, they watched as the luka lifted one dark wing in self-protection and hobbled back into the shadows.

The group was quiet for a long moment. Then they looked at

each other, still panting, their hearts still pounding.

Mekial found his voice first. "That…was…*awesome!*"

Brent smiled crookedly, still just a tad out of breath.

Harver gripped her knees, relieved. "I thought we were goners!"

"Good thing we brought Taranis' best with us!" Eklaire added, looking at Liam, Brent and Renée.

"Good thing it's still light out, too," Liam added. "We're lucky that luka prefer the dark. Shouldn't bother us anymore."

"That was so cool!" Mekial cried. "With Liam throwing the smoke-bomb like 'hoo-yah!' and then Ren was all like" — he pretended to bite something and threw an invisible object — "'hyah!' and I almost stabbed it —"

"You almost got yourself killed," Renée interrupted sternly and at the edge of their gathering, Brent started to look around. "I told you this place was dangerous! You could've gotten really hurt!"

"Yeah, but I'm *not* hurt…"

"Mekial, you're too reckless!"

"Did we go all the way through the cave?" Brent asked quietly, looking out into the plains beyond. "This is the back entrance."

"Looks like we did," Liam joined as the others kept conversing.

There was no meandering road that would lead them back to Taranis, only a hooded and small field enclosed by foothills and a spattering of trees. Straight ahead in the distance, if Brent wasn't mistaken, was the Arkanian Prune plateau, while behind them there was a path that climbed through a forest of thin birches before it descended behind the next hill. If his memory served correctly, which he was sure that it did, the path wound back to the entrance of Heletia Cavern, where the same road that they'd traveled from Taranis would be waiting to guide them back home.

"This is perfect!" Harver exclaimed suddenly, looking around. "If we hadn't come out this way, I would've totally forgotten that there was one more thing I needed to get!"

"What's that?" Brent asked.

"A qazhë flower," she answered.

"Qazhë?" Brent translated the word from Aionbo. "A wind flower?"

"They're common around this area," Harver went on, after she'd nodded in answer to him. "Only, since they have a bulbous shape and they're also green, they're kind of hard to locate."

If any of them were to find one, they were to flick its husk lightly, she added as an instruction. That would encourage the flower to unravel and reveal a cluster of hollow white seeds, which was what she needed the most.

"And don't eat them," she finished tiredly, as if she'd had to explain that once before to someone who hadn't listened.

"They're poisonous if you eat them, we know," Mekial said. "Don't worry."

"What exactly do you need those seeds for, anyway?" Renée asked curiously as Brent and Liam set Harver's supplies down again.

"It's a secret!" Harver put a finger to her lips. "For my invention."

"Y'know, you *still* haven't told us what your invention is," Brent pointed out. "Why not?"

"Because it's a secret!" Harver repeated. "But when it's done, you raiders'll never be raiding the same way again!"

"So you've been saying for the past year."

"Well, it's true. Now let's get looking already, it'll be dark soon!"

Figuring that they wouldn't get any more details out of her, they all spread out in search of her requested plant. Again they divided into groups, halving their party first, then dwindling down to teams of two until eventually they were searching individually, though not so far apart that they couldn't look up and spot each other.

But, as common as the qazhë flower was to the wooded area outside of Heletia Cavern's western entrance, that didn't make it any easier to find. More often than not, they laid eyes on regular weeds or other such plants.

Once, Mekial thought he found it and hollered for everyone's attention victoriously.

But then he realized that it was just a wildflower.

"False alarm!" he called out.

"This is almost crazy," Eklaire said, bending down to peer between the leaves of a soft bush. "I feel like they're hidin' from us!"

"There's gotta be one around here somewhere," Renée said from behind her, rising from having examined the base of a thick tree.

"I'm sure one of us'll find it soon."

Away from them, Harver let loose a loud and dramatic gasp.

"Did you find it?!" Brent whirled to see her. He was nearer to the clearing that opened into the neighboring field, opposite Renée, Mekial and Eklaire. Harver was close by him, crouching a few trees away, and Liam wasn't too far from her.

"I found something *better!*" she squealed and she jumped to her feet, her cheeks in her hands. "It's a gourd root!"

Brent went to see what she was talking about.

Liam simply turned from his study of a windmill-shaped flower.

The gourd root, as Harver called it, was in fact shaped like a gourd, with a husk that was a gradient mix of red and yellow. Its mouth was just as fiery, with a fan of bright red flower petals and yellow stamens surrounding it, while an array of matching pistils encased its body.

Prompted by curiosity, Brent peeked inside of it: its insides were completely black.

And bubbling.

He furrowed an eyebrow.

"The gourd root is filled with a naturally acidic mucus that can be used as an adhesive when it's mixed with a less-acidic chemical!" Harver exclaimed.

Brent's brow puckered even more. "Like what?"

"Spit." Harver cleared her throat and then, squinting one eye, she made one long, loud hocking sound, like she was getting ready to launch a big one.

Just before she could fire her missile, Liam clapped his hand over her mouth.

Her big eyes went up to his face. Then, she swallowed loudly — as she did her eyes crossed and she shook a little.

"Stay quiet," he said. His eyes weren't on her but with his head tilted as they shifted back and forth, she could tell that he was focused less on his sight and more on his hearing, which had seemed to just tune in to something.

Once sure that she'd quieted herself his hand fell from her mouth, and he slowly turned to face a nearby cluster of trees. They were sandwiched between the cave that they'd just exited and another mountain.

Harver cautiously turned to look in the same direction.

Brent mimicked her.

The sound that she and Liam could hear at a decent volume wasn't too loud in his ears, but he knew that it wasn't yet close enough for Renée, Mekial or Eklaire to pick up on. It sounded like something was charging in their direction.

And it was big.

"Mekial," Renée said distantly, noticing how stiff the other half of their party had become. "Take Eklaire and find cover." One hand on the hilt of her sword, she hurried away.

The boy ran over to Eklaire. "What's wrong?"

She simply shrugged.

"Fall back, Harver," Brent said to her, his eyes never leaving the trees.

Harver's dark eyes flitted between him and Liam. "B-but…"

"We'll be fine." Brent flashed her a confident smile. "This is our job as the escort, remember?"

Harver hesitated for a second, and then she nodded. Turning, she jogged away just as Renée crossed over to take her place.

Eklaire and Mekial went to meet her.

The rumbling that Harver had heard was much closer now, bringing with it the resounding crash of trees groaning feebly as they toppled over. Closer to the destruction, a swarm of birds took to the skies in fright.

"What's going on?" Mekial nervously watched the creatures fly away and disappear over the valley.

Harver whipped around to see them as well, and at the same time the approach of whatever was nearing them grew louder, magnifying until the very earth rumbled beneath its weight.

Following its sound to the source, her dark eyes leveled with the trees.

There, an enormous black figure was racing towards them, barreling straight through rocks and boughs as if they weren't even there. At last and with a thunderous crash, it roared into the clearing with enough force to send a storm of branches flying.

It was an entelodon.

But it was far larger than any entelodon that any of them had ever seen, larger even than the one that Brent had killed the previous summer. Compared to that one, this beast appeared to be fully grown: two long tusks jutted out of the sides of its mouth with two slightly shorter ones flanking them, and a single, gigantic horn curved out of its face. Its beady little eyes burned with fury and as its muscular body heaved with heavy gasps, steam practically spewed from its four flared nostrils. Fangs the width of a man's waist were visible through the furry bristles that lined its mouth.

Liam actually blinked in surprise.

Renée's mouth fell open.

Brent's eyes bulged and the Katruskan tongue left him. *"Nilb."*

55

THE ENTELODON ROARED, shaking the air, and Brent, Liam and Renée shielded themselves against its foul breath.

When its cry finally ended, they looked at each other.

Then, they ran away.

"I thought this was your job!" Harver shouted when she saw them sprinting out of the clearing and towards the tree-lined path that was behind her.

"I think we can make an exception this time!" Brent yelled back. *"Run!"*

The entelodon bellowed again and it started running, kicking up grass in place before it actually started to pursue.

Harver, Mekial and Eklaire were already alongside Brent and the others by the time that it did. But when they reached the top of the path, Harver stopped and looked back fearfully.

"Wait!" she cried. "My supplies!"

Ahead of her Brent skidded to a stop and looked at Harver's bags, then at the entelodon.

It was only a matter of time before it ran the whole pile over.

"It'll take us weeks to replace it all!" she wailed, grabbing her head.

Brent's mind raced, hitting him with a series of bullet-pointed thoughts. He realized one thing first:

There was no way they were outrunning this monster.

"Mekial, stay with Eklaire and Harver!" he shouted. "Ren, Liam, let's go!" He ran at the boar and with grim faces, Renée and Liam went after him.

Brent and Liam reached Harver's bags before the entelodon could and grabbed them both. Ripping them out of the beast's way, they narrowly avoided the hairy brute when it swung its tusks at them.

Spinning back around, it unleashed a hoarse roar.

Brent thrust his arm into Harver's shoulder bag and ripped out what he understood to be a modified grappling hook: the cord was thick and durable but it still had a certain elasticity, while the grappling bit was more of a hooked blade.

Dumping the bag, he tossed the cord to Renée. "Renée, blind it!"

"Got it!" Catching the item, she whirled it like a lasso and ran at the entelodon.

Huffing brilliantly, it charged at her with its horn low.

Whipping her arm across the air, Renée loosed the hooked blade so that it could arc into the entelodon's left eye.

Her aim was true, and the beast stopped to release a horrible scream when the knife crashed into its eyeball.

Tugging on the cord, Renée slid to a stop and yanked the knife back out.

Again the entelodon squealed, its head flying back in pain.

Swinging and arcing the cord while it was still in midair, Renée sent the knife crashing into its right eye next.

Her aim was just as perfect.

With the world now lost to it, the entelodon let out a bloodcurdling screech that tumbled across the fields.

Renée tore the knife out again, pulling the weapon back to herself just as the creature swung its head in anguish. She snatched it when it was close.

The beast continued to scream and wail, its head swinging wildly. With a heavy snarl, it started running into the fields.

"Toss me the rope!" Brent yelled, sprinting to a spot across from Renée. "Loop your part around that tree!"

Seeing the tree that he'd indicated, which was just behind her, Renée ran to it. At the same time she wound her arm back and threw part of the rope to him.

He caught it and wrapped it around the wide trunk of a chestnut tree that he'd already been running to. Stretching the rope around it he gripped it with both hands, braced one foot against the trunk, and twisted the other into the earth.

"Pull!" he roared, hauling on the rope, and with one foot pressed against the trunk that was near her, Renée stretched her side of the cord just as taut. She bared her teeth with the effort, her brow knotting and muscles flexing.

Completely blind, the entelodon didn't see the taut stretch of rope that was rising to block its path. So with a scream, it stumbled over the obstacle and skidded face-first into the ground.

The cord itself snapped and Brent winced as he backpedaled, his balance almost lost. He whirled around.

"Liam, go!" he yelled roughly.

Liam, who'd been waiting only a few yards ahead of where the entelodon was at that moment, drew his blade and charged. Skipping atop the beast's snout and rounding its horn, he stood at the crest of its nape and lifted his blade. Knees buckling, he stabbed the entelodon's skull.

Screeching, it reared onto its feet.

Liam clutched both his sword and the hairs of the brute's neck to keep from being flung to the ground. Flattening onto his stomach, he held on tight as the monster shook its head and bounded and bucked, rattling the ground with every jump.

Brent hastily began to rethink their strategy.

Blind, pained and frustrated, the entelodon charged in his direction with its horn lowered.

But Brent sidestepped it, and he jumped out of range completely when the force behind the beast made it bury its snout into the ground again.

Right when it made to round on him once more, Renée appeared at its side. Driving the tip of her sword into the ground she flung it up, spraying one of its bloody eyes with a curtain of grass and soil.

HARDER THEY FALL
CODE: NEWSPECIES

Tearing its face out of the ground, it roared vengefully.

Up on its head, Liam unsheathed his sword from the beast's skin and leaped off, landing near Renée.

"Its got a thick hide," he said. "Don't think I got through to anything."

Overcoming the dirt that Renée had used to irritate its wound, the entelodon's four nostrils widened and it shortly sniffed the air. Then, dipping its head, it bellowed mightily in Brent's face.

Gritting his teeth, he bowed his head and shielded himself with his arms, his heels digging into the dirt. Webs of spit blew past him.

"Brent!" Renée shouted, and she ran to offer him support. Sliding in front of him, she slashed at the boar's face.

It swung its head away in rage.*tv*

Up the road, Harver's face lit up with an idea and she ran for her backpack.

"Harver!" Eklaire reached out to stop her, as did Mekial.

But she went too fast.

While Brent and the others ducked and dodged around the boar and its mindlessly swinging tusks, Harver dropped to her knees and slid towards her backpack. Throwing it open, she looked at what was inside: flash orbs, a couple of spyglasses, some smoke sticks, a compass…

She started digging through it all.

"Any new ideas, Brent?!" Renée shouted, jumping out of the way of one of the entelodon's tusk-attacks. She rolled to safety but before she could get back to her feet, the beast's head came swinging back around.

Her eyes widened in petrified shock before she got the sense to duck.

The entelodon's head rushed over her, making her hair and feather piece flutter like mad.

"Got it!" Harver pulled a small black ball out of her bag triumphantly.

Grinning, she looked at her friends, only to have her face fall when Liam dodged the entelodon's next rush and inadvertently left Harver as its only target.

But before it could ram into her, someone else blocked its path and swiped the black sphere from her hand.

At the same time, the entelodon's hairy snout caught her rescuer and threw him into the sky.

Renée looked to see who'd been hit. Her eyes bulged. *"Mekial!"*

Up in the air the boy's face was scrunched up, pained by the strength of the creature's impact on his abdomen. Still, he managed to push through and squint down at it: it looked a lot smaller now that he was flying so high up.

And then, he started to fall.

Working fast, he ripped a plug out of the ball that he'd snatched from Harver. With a grunt, he threw it at the entelodon with all of his strength.

The ball whistled shrilly as it descended, and right when it was near the beast's head it erupted in an explosive blast of fire and smoke.

Caught in the detonation the entelodon teetered, its jaw going slack as it fell out of the smoke. When it crashed to the ground, the earth trembled with the might of a small earthquake.

Everyone stared at the fallen beast, shocked. Only Mekial's yelling snapped them out of their trances.

"Somebody catch me!" he cried as he plummeted, his arms and legs flailing.

Speedily calculating the boy's landing spot Brent started towards him, jogging first, then running. He dove to catch him.

He twisted onto his side at the same time, offsetting the force behind Mekial's weight, and as he skidded across the road clouds of dirt choked the air.

Renée sheathed her sword and ran to them. "Are you guys all right?!"

"O-ow…" Mekial rolled out of Brent's arms and sat up. "That thing…hits *hard*…"

Renée knelt down next to him, one hand on his head. Her eyes went to Brent next.

He grunted as he sat up and brushed some loose dirt and pebbles off of his arm. His skin was scraped in some places but other than that, he seemed fine.

"You okay?" she asked.

"Nothin' bad." He looked at Mekial. "But I thought I told you to stay back."

"You said to stay with Harver and Eklaire," Mekial reminded him. "But Harver would've gotten trampled if I hadn't jumped in! You're welcome."

Brent's eyes soundlessly darted to Renée.

"From what I could tell, he did save her," she said. "Even if he was being reckless."

"Says the raider who charged headlong at an entelodon because Brent told her to," Mekial quipped. He smiled slyly at the red that entered his sister's cheeks. "I'm telling Mom."

Renée composed herself. "Hey, you did the same thing! At least I didn't end up getting booted into the sky."

Mekial turned away with a dull scoff.

"She's right, man." Brent stood and offered a hand to help the boy up. "You're a little too reckless. Like with the luka? You could've gotten hurt way worse than you are now."

"Yeah, but…" Mekial stared at the ground after taking Brent's offer. He kept one hand on his stomach. "I wanted to help. *You guys* run into danger!"

"We were trained for it, though." Renée bent forward to look him in the eye. She put a hand on his scruffy head of hair. "You're not exactly ready for any of that just yet."

Eyebrows furrowed, Mekial wouldn't look at her.

Renée righted herself with a gentle sigh.

"Your sister's just worried about you, Mek," Brent said to the boy. "We know you're tough. But you're gonna have to slow down a bit. If you get wrecked as a trainee, you won't get to help any of the slaves."

Mekial scowled, but he understood.

"Then you'll end up with a lame outlaw name," Brent went on with a boyish grin. "Like Ren!"

Renée started. "Hey, I didn't even get one yet!"

"You're right. My bad, Madame Fuddy-Duddy."

Renée groaned and face-palmed.

Mekial laughed.

"What the heck was that explosion?" Eklaire asked as she circled closer to the battlesite. From a safe distance she leaned forward to study the entelodon's dead body, which was surrounded by soot and smoldering cinders.

"It was a new tool for the raiders. A prototype, really." Harver stood up, dusted her clothes off and hopped over her bag to get a better look at the beast. "There's no name for it yet. For now, it's just a stronger bomb with a bit of a delay. Still…" Her face saddened. "This guy didn't need to die so horribly."

Eklaire observed the entelodon's marred face with a similarly upset look.

Liam looked at the bloody carcass with them. "Better it than us."

Harver twisted her lip in silent agreement. "I wonder why it was coming after us at all, though." Kneeling beside it, she touched its still face.

"Hmm, y'know…" Eklaire cocked her head and squinted a bit. "It kinda reminds me of the one ya'll hunted for last year's Feast!" She looked at Liam, implying that she was speaking to him. "Just, well, bigger."

Sheathing his sword, Liam looked the creature over again.

"Because it is," Harver realized. "The tusks are fully grown and there're more of them. Not to mention its size…" She looked at Liam. "I think it could be an older member of the same herd. But…" She frowned, puzzled, and observed the entelodon again. "Why would another one show up now?" She lifted her head when Brent, Mekial and Renée joined them.

"Everyone all right?" Brent asked, looking them all over. "Harver?"

"I'm fine," she said, standing. "But Mekial, what about you? You took a pretty hard hit."

"Ah, it was nothin'! I've been working out!" He patted his stomach and instantly regretted it. "Ow…!"

"Easy there, Mekial," Renée said, her hand going to his shoulder as he doubled over. "We should have Khirsta check you out. You might've broken something."

Mekial just grimaced in uncomfortable silence, still rubbing his stomach.

"The explosion?" Brent looked at Harver.

"Prototype for a new bomb," Liam said.

"Prototype…so it's not in our arsenal yet." Brent looked at Mekial and his sister. "How'd Mek know how to use it?"

"The trainees went to the engineers' workshop yesterday to learn about the tools they might someday use on missions," Renée explained as Mekial struggled to recover from his self-inflicted pain. "He was told about it there."

"Huh."

"…Brent," Harver drew his eye, and he noticed her grim expression, "I don't think this entelodon was on a wild rampage. It seemed to know what it was after."

"What was that?" he asked.

"I think…" She hesitated. "I think it wanted *you.*"

Brent raised his eyebrows.

"How d'you figure?" Liam asked.

"For one thing, entelodons always find things by tracking their scent." Harver looked at him. "That can be prey, or a relative that was separated from its herd. This one was sniffing the air a lot and it's foreign to the valley, maybe even to the lowlands where the entelodons tend to wander in from. The only time we've ever seen anything like it was when you killed that huge one for the Feast last year."

"What're you saying, Harver?" Brent crossed his arms over his bare chest. His flat tone insisted that he wanted her to get to the point.

Harver sensed it. "I think this entelodon was related to that one," she said decidedly. "Somehow they got separated, so it started to search for it. But, at some point it…might've smelled blood instead."

Brent's eyes narrowed with solemn understanding. "On me."

Harver shifted a little, her brow creasing with remorse. Then, she nodded.

Renée looked at Brent concernedly.

He didn't meet her gaze.

"So, y'mean to say that this entelodon's been lookin' fer its relative fer the past *year?*" Eklaire pointed at the beast in surprise.

"The entelodons that we usually see are extremely sentimental, Eklaire," Harver replied. "While this one definitely doesn't look like them exactly, it's probably a closely related species. I'm sure they have the same traits." She turned to examine the deceased animal again and her forehead wrinkled a little. "…I wonder if it was a parent."

Eklaire's shoulders slumped in dismay.

Liam took the liberty of breaking the silence. "Whether or not that's true, we can't have its body taking up the whole road like this," he said. "For now, we have to finish what we were doing. When we get back to Taranis, I'll find some aetheriests and have them move it."

"Right." Brent unfolded his arms. He appeared distracted. "Good idea."

Harver's eyes fell despairingly. At the same time, she spotted a dark green object that she hadn't noticed before.

It was a qazhë flower, its bell-shaped form visible from the road only because the tree that had pressed it against a bush had been struck by the entelodon. It was a wonder it hadn't been crushed.

Gasping excitedly she ran to it, causing her friends to watch her in question.

Ignoring them she dropped to her knees in front of the flower and leaned towards it, clapping her hands together as if in prayer.

"Please be ripe…!" she whispered and, lifting a hand, she flicked the flower's closed petals.

It shuddered and then, gracefully, it unfurled itself in a backwards spiral, unveiling a yellow interior that was speckled with tiny, orange polka-dots. Clinging to its very center was a cluster of white seeds, each the size of a grape.

"Yes!" Beaming, she plucked them free.

"That's it?" Renée walked over to get a better look. Bending forward with her hands on her knees, she eyed the seeds curiously.

"What do you mean, 'that's it'?" Harver rose to her feet, seeds in hand. "Just wait 'til you see what I make these babies do!"

"Huh…y'know, they don't even look poisonous," Eklaire observed as Harver returned to the group, smiling at her new ingredients. "They're actually kinda pretty!"

"Do you have a secure place for them?" Renée asked and in response, Harver slipped a small pouch out of her pocket.

"Way ahead of ya." Dropping the qazhë seeds into the little bag, she pulled the drawstring tight to close it. "Now we've got everything!"

"Then it looks like it's time to head back." Liam went to retrieve Harver's bags.

Brent moved to assist.

Harver and Eklaire followed them and as they walked away, Renée tried to catch Brent's eye.

He didn't look at her.

"My body's gonna kill for days…" Mekial groaned, and he moved away from his sister to join them on their return to the village.

Renée trailed after him slowly and as she came nearer to the group, she noticed the remote frown that Brent's face had settled into.

Her brow creased gently.

Picking up speed, she moved closer to him.

"Brent," she called and he stopped, turning to see her.

She held his gaze, her own soft with empathy. Over his shoulder and out of her peripheral, their friends started up the hill. "Are you okay?"

He faced her fully, curious now. "Sure. Why?"

Renée's eyebrows puckered ever so slightly. "Well, after what Harver just said…" She came nearer to him. "I just" — she smiled quickly, genuinely, and stopped a few paces before him — "wanted to make sure that you're all right."

His lips twitched into a half-smile. "Thanks. Guess I can't completely hide it." He looked back to see their departing friends. Harver was already scolding Liam for the way that he was carrying her backpack, to which he calmly adjusted the straps to her liking as he went along. When Eklaire said something in response, Harver immediately blushed and flailed, leaving Mekial and the Lenoran in stitches. "Not everyday you find out a herd of entelodon might be holding a grudge against you. Not like it can be helped…"

"Because sometimes 'it takes an entelodon to feed a village'."

Brent looked back at Renée, his eyebrows raised.

She smiled with a knowing tilt of her head. "Right?"

To this his surprise faded and his expression lightened. "Took the words right out of my mouth. Does kinda suck for the entelodons, though."

Renée's laugh was a quiet one, a light whisper against the wind. "Well, even if Harver was right about them, it's only because you're concerned about the people of Taranis and making sure that they're well-fed. That may look cold and heartless to an entelodon, since we hunt them…" She came nearer, her eyes lowering, and she placed her hand over his heart. "But to the rest of us, it just means that you have a heart for others." She looked up at him, the sides of her mouth drawn high and her eyes warm. "Don't ever lose that."

Brent hadn't meant to stare at her for as long as he did. Or perhaps it hadn't been that long at all. He always seemed to lose track of the most basic of things in moments like this, when she was this close.

So it had to be instinct, or perhaps even his subconscious, that led him to raise his own hand and close it over hers. Stepping closer, he answered with gentle confidence. "I won't."

"Guys, hurry up!" Harver suddenly called back to them, realizing that they were lagging. "We gotta get back before nightfall!"

"We're coming!" Renée shouted and she smiled up at Brent one last time before stepping away from him.

Thus her hand slid out of his.

Twisting on his heel, he caught it again. "Wait!"

She looked back. This time, it was her turn to be curious.

"Uh, I mean…" Letting her go, he scratched the back of his head. "Just…thanks."

She giggled quietly. "You know, I think I should be the one thanking you."

Brent's confusion was evident. "For what?"

"For talking to Mekial earlier. Between you, Aaron and Liam, he looks up to you the most. What you said'll stick better that way."

"I only told him what Jeffrey always told us," he said. "'If you just throw yourself at your enemy's sword' —"

"'Then who's gonna protect the slaves you're supposed to rescue?'" Renée finished the quote.

Brent smiled softly.

"C'mon, you guys!" Harver yelled. "Are you making out down there or something?! We're burning daylight, hurry it up!"

"Eww, you're making out?!" Mekial spiraled. "That's my sister!"

Heat rushed to Brent's cheeks.

Renée herself turned scarlet.

Their eyes met for half a second before they both turned away.

Pulling her hair over her shoulder, Renée started playing with it.

"Well, come on already!" Harver waved as the others continued on. "I gotta get this stuff back to my workshop!"

The next exchange of glances that Brent and Renée shared were short and bashful. With a motion of his arm, Brent gestured for her to head up the road first.

Still playing with her hair, she accepted the offer.

Behind her, Brent blew some air out of his mouth quietly, then followed. As for the frown that had grayed his face before Renée's approach, it was entirely gone.

Still, someplace far beneath it, a memory lay dormant: one where a woman had passed away in a wagon, and the man that had wept for her had blamed it on a child.

Yes…certainly, Brent was no stranger to grudges.

⚮

It was nearing sunset when they made it back to Taranis, and shortly after their arrival Liam separated from their party. As he'd said before, he intended to gather some aetheriests and return to Heletia Cavern to take care of the entelodon.

Renée meant to part with the group as well and bring Mekial to see Khirsta. But when her brother oddly insisted that he was fine enough to go alone later, she relented.

So the two of them accompanied the rest of their friends to Harver's house, where they helped drop off her belongings at her workshop. It was almost a mission in and of itself to find a place to put her bulging bags and new supplies, but eventually they picked a spot in one of the corners that wasn't as chaotic as everywhere else.

After thanking them Harver stated that she'd remain in the shop, saying that she wanted to start working on upgrading a prototype for her project.

Respecting her choice, her friends bid her farewell and returned to the main road, where they ran into Liam once more.

He had a few aetheriests with him, and they were just about to leave for Heletia to retrieve the entelodon. Upon learning this, Brent offered to join them.

Right as they were about to leave, Renée moved as if to say something to him.

He noticed. "It's all good, Ren. This one'll probably take care of the people in the apartments for the next week!"

At this the girl stepped back, at ease. She smiled. "You bet!"

Winking, he left, trekking into the farmlands to join with Liam and the others.

As they went, Eklaire stretched her arms high over her head. "Hoooo-*whee!* What a day this has been! Too bad Aaron had to miss out. It's a dern shame — that boy sure does love to be a part of the action! Or else he'll just make his own."

"Yeah…" Renée frowned and set her sights on the valley. "I wonder where he went this time."

"Maybe up to Gilead? Or all the way to Orinn?" Eklaire thought, looking out into the vale with her. She turned to her friend. "But whatever he's up to now, I doubt it could match what we just had to deal with. Heletia's rarely dangerous. He missed the adventure of a lifetime!"

Renée couldn't help but give a light laugh. "You hardly seem freaked out by any of it."

"Are you kiddin'? I've been holed up with all the other seamstresses fer days, makin' new clothes for kids, or newborns, or repairin' sashes'n stuff. All those close calls really got my blood pumpin'! Matter of fact, I think I mighta got a new idea or two after runnin' around in there. Keep yer eyes peeled fer new merch from Eklaire Dunbar's Good Ol'-Fashioned Fashion Front!" She smiled brightly.

Renée laughed. "You're always an optimist, Eklaire."

"Can't help it! But, I'll admit it was a lil' scary at times. I like to have died when that luka broke 'round the corner'n Mekial ran screamin' at it!"

"Which reminds me," Renée turned to her brother. "You're still going to Khirsta's, right?"

"Yeah, I'll go…" Mekial stroked his stomach and took a backward step up the main road.

"Sure you don't need me to come with you?"

"I'll be okay!" he said, hardly losing his insistence from earlier, and he started up the main road. "I'll just go now. I'll see you at home."

"Okay." Though she agreed, Renée's discomfort was obvious.

Eklaire noticed. "I know what yer thinkin'."

Renée looked at her, her innocent expression denoting a certain lack of awareness. "What?"

"Yer worried he's gonna collapse halfway up the hill!"

"Well, I mean…he got tossed by an *entelodon*. How am I supposed to feel?"

"Yeah, I know. I saw it, too! Can't say I'm not worried 'bout the lil' guy myself. But I'm sure Khirsta'll take a look at him, wrap him up and he'll be all right. He seems fine now, though. Kinda odd…"

Renée didn't appear to be delighted by that observation.

"Still, maybe you oughta give the boy some credit." Eklaire watched her with a sympathetic smile. "He is followin' in your shoes, and Terra's shoes, and Ben's shoes…" She glanced out to the road winding away from Taranis. "Even Brent's shoes!"

"I just don't want him to be careless. He could get really hurt. What if the entelodon's horn had gored him?" Renée hugged herself. "If that had happened, I'd…"

Eklaire walked to a spot directly in front of her and planted her hands on Renée's shoulders. She took a deep breath.

"*Relax!*" she yelled.

Renée jumped, bug-eyed.

"Mekial ain't gonna be actin' a fool forever. He's got way too much good counsel!" Eklaire let go of her, her eyes alight. "And so long as he's got you for a sister, Terra for a mama and Ben'n Jeffrey to keep him in line, he'll turn out okay! But if it makes ya feel any better" — she shook her fist — "I could jerk a knot in his tail for ya! Get him back fer makin' his pretty sister age twenty years in two minutes."

Renée's laughter was light, but truthful. "I might take you up on that."

"Just give the word! Why d'you think I'm one of the best babysitters in all of Taranis, anyway? Even Lilian knows how to act right when I'm around. And that lil' darlin' — bless her heart — she can be such a *handful!*" Eklaire's shoulders sagged, her eyes wide as she actually considered their friend's energetic niece. "Sometimes I don't know how Liam does it."

"He probably just does a good job of hiding his stress."

Eklaire giggled. "The deadpan look secretly hides his achin' soul."

They both laughed, their voices a chime of joy that added just a dash more light to their peaceful home.

"There it is!" Eklaire beamed as Renée wiped her eye. "The good ol' Ren Smile!"

Renée smiled gratefully. "Thanks, Eklaire."

Her friend grinned. "Anytime!"

"And what do we have here, hmm? A girls' night out?"

Renée and Eklaire turned to one of the side roads that opened out onto the main hill, and were surprised to see Xëri walking towards them.

"Lady Xëri!" Renée greeted, her startled expression playing into her voice.

"Heya, Lady Xëri!" Eklaire chimed in, waving.

"Good evening to you both." Xëri paused in front of them. "I heard Liam going around looking for aetheriests a little while ago. Is everything all right?"

"Oh, totally! Mostly." Eklaire considered for a second. "Sorta."

"We had a run-in with an entelodon after taking Harver to Heletia Cavern," Renée explained. "Liam and Brent are leading some aetheriests to the body, so they can get it off the road."

"Oh, so we're having entelodon meat again, huh?" Xëri sighed. "I think I'll have to look into some new ways to cook up their ribs. Maybe I'll try roasting them in that sauce tonight…"

"Just the ribs?" Eklaire asked.

"Well, those are Chief Ivan's favorite part," the woman admitted. "Brent and Aaron have always been suckers for the steak tips themselves."

"Steak tips, huh?" Renée repeated quietly.

Eklaire overheard her. "Maybe you should take up a cookin' lesson with Lady Xëri! Y'know what they say: the fastest way to a man's heart is through his stomach! I'm sure Brent'd appreciate the surprise."

Renée's face turned red. "I wasn't — I didn't — " She rounded on Xëri. "I wasn't thinking about that!"

Xëri laughed, genuinely entertained. "It's all right. He's a charming boy. I wouldn't have been surprised. And you're a charming girl, so I wouldn't have minded it at all."

Renée blushed harder.

"Brent's charisma draws people to him," Xëi remarked. "He's got an air of mystery about him, too."

"Yeah…" Renée calmed down a little, solemn. "I've noticed that."

Eklaire watched her curiously.

"A lot more recently, at least," Renée continued. "He always marches around Taranis with that big grin of his, and he's always helping someone or playing with the kids. But, sometimes, he seems distracted. And…sad."

"He's been through a lot," Xëri told her, her own face falling. "As have so many others who've come here over the years."

Neither Renée nor Eklaire had anything to say to that, though their expressions did show that they understood the truth of what Xëri had said.

"He thinks quite highly of you though, Renée." Xëri's face softened.

Eklaire covered her mouth in surprise and excitement.

Renée seemed caught off guard. "He does?"

"You're one of the people who inspired him to become an auction raider," Xëri clarified.

Renée's astonishment soon melted away. "To be honest, I don't feel like much of an inspiration. It feels like there's been a standstill since I graduated. I can't even remember the last time that I heard about a scout reaching out to us."

"That's true. But don't discount your character."

Renée's face became questioning.

Xëri smiled. "There's a lot more to you than your ambition to save the slaves. And from what I've heard Brent say, there's a lot more about you that he holds in high respect. I think that much holds true for all of your underclassmen at the sparring hall, too."

"Oh…" Renée felt her face heat up all over again.

"I wouldn't worry too much about the scouts either, at least not now. Chief Ivan's got someone looking into it. As for who," she added, noticing Eklaire's mouth opening, "I can't say."

Eklaire deflated. "Booo…"

Xëri smiled. "It's actually good that I ran into you, Eklaire. It's been too long since I saw Isabel, what with all the work I've been doing these past few weeks, so I was thinking to visit. Did you want to join us? Or are we too old to be graced by the company of such beautiful young women?" A playful light entered her eye. "Will our wrinkles rub off on you? We too outdated, maybe?"

"No way!" Eklaire grew elated. "Why not come over?! I'm sure Mama's done with work! And after all that hustlin' around, I could go for somethin' sweet to take the edge off. How 'bout you, Ren?"

She nodded. "Yeah. Sounds good."

"I'll say. You look worn slap-out. Tell you what, I'll bake you somethin' special myself! Well, what're we waitin' for?! To my house we go!" Swinging her arm in the direction of her home across the stream, Eklaire started marching towards it.

Xëri and Renée followed, with the chief's wife sliding Renée a gentle smile as she went along.

Renée returned it and soon looked into the valley again, towards the road that plowed towards Heletia Cavern.

She couldn't see Brent, Liam or the aetheriests anymore. But she considered Xëri's words, and smiled.

56

I DON'T SEE ANYTHING wrong. There's hardly a bruise." Khirsta straightened up from her examination of Mekial's stomach, her wrinkled face pulling into a smile.

She was a short Avat woman, barely taller than he was, and her thick gray hair had a dark streak shooting through it. A jeweled hairpin held it in a high bun, and finely woven patterns adorned her clothes.

She lived at the top of the main road in a one-room hut that was diagonal to the Main House. It was a small place, with a kitchen to the right of the doorway and two beds towards the back, one of which Mekial was presently sitting on. The other was behind a patterned curtain at his back.

Several intricate rugs and tasseled tapestries decorated the rest of her home, along with a shelf of medicinal herbs and potions. A table littered with herbs, berries and powders was just beneath it, further emphasizing her trade of healing and medicine, and they saturated the abode with a sweet, earthy aroma.

"Perhaps someone is watching over you." Khirsta made her way over to a mortar and pestle that was on the table, meaning to return to the work she'd been doing before Mekial had burst in on her.

"It hurt like crazy earlier…" Mekial mumbled, looking at his stomach over his rolled up shirt. As Khirsta had said, there was no bruise. It was as if he'd never been struck by the entelodon at all. "Ren kept wanting me to come see you, but by the time we got back to Taranis I was feeling completely fine." He pulled his shirt down. "I didn't wanna make her freak out more, so I didn't tell her."

"Interesting." Khirsta's earrings and other loose jewelry jangled as she ground her herbs, but she soon stopped to look at him. "And this beast was large?"

"It was huge!" Mekial spread his arms for emphasis. "Ren said something might've been broken, and I think I remember feeling like something had cracked, but…" He rubbed his stomach. "The pain's all gone now. Am I weird?"

Khirsta's thin, almond-shaped eyes crinkled as she laughed. Her wrinkles became more prominent, testifying to her age, but one could tell that her high cheekbones had likely been the more dominant and attractive feature in her youth. "No, child. You're not weird."

"But then why wouldn't I have like…I dunno, snapped in half?"

"I'm not sure." Khirsta cocked her head thoughtfully. "The only time I've ever seen something like this is when an aetheriest increases his quintessence and expels it as a shield around himself, to protect himself from an attack."

"But…I didn't conjure up a shield or anything. At least…" Mekial pondered for a second. "I don't *think* I did…Mom, Dad and Ren used to think I was an aetheriest." He looked up. "They said I used to be able to do weird things when I was little, but then every time I went to Heldar I wouldn't be able to do anything all of a sudden. Eventually I decided to sign up for Jeffrey's classes, like Ren did, cuz I felt like I could actually do something there. But…" He frowned distractedly, a hand on his belly. "This is still weird…"

"Sounds like a mystery." Despite the ominous words chosen, Khirsta's smile was warm. "Still, I'm glad you're all right."

"Yeah." Mekial hopped off the bed. "Same here."

"I would recommend seeing Heldar or one of the aetheriests again at least," Khirsta offered as Mekial took a step towards the doorway. "Perhaps they can offer some input on what actually happened."

"Yeah…good idea." Mekial frowned thoughtfully before giving her a quick nod. "Thanks, Khirsta. Bye!" He flicked his hand up in a wave and left rather hurriedly without looking back.

Was he an aetheriest?

No, that didn't make any sense, he thought next. While anyone, aside from Avats, was capable of becoming an aetheriest, no one could become one without the proper training. And he'd never been trained before.

But, he supposed that there had to be someone in Taranis that he could ask for advice.

He hurried for the apartments.

✢

Alone in the conference room of the Main House, Ivan traced his finger across the map that was spread out on the table, drawing an invisible line from the province of Lyrik to the southern coasts of Lenora. He paused at Aiken, a coastal trading city, before he dragged his fingertip into the ocean.

"Is such a far journey," he thought aloud, leaning away from the detailed, geographical illustration. "Is impressive…"

All at once, the door clicked open and an Avat man stepped inside.

He was a somber character, middle-aged, with jet-black hair that was slicked into a half-ponytail. Behind him, Ivan could see beams of red light that were likely stemming through the windows of the dining hall, signifying the nearing hour of dusk. The rich, herbal scent of roasted proardea and entelodon also wafted through the air.

"Yuan." Ivan greeted the man who'd entered with a dip of his chin.

"Chief." His assistant repeated the motion. The sunset's burning glow gave his dark eyes a level of unmatched intensity. "He's back."

Hardly a moment later, Yuan was gone and Aaron was standing in his place.

He was muddied and ragged, and one of the first things Ivan

noticed was that he wasn't wearing the same cowl that he'd donned upon his departure several days ago. Instead he was wearing a silken bandana, and a new traveler's cloak was wrapped around his shoulders. He'd also acquired a broadsword.

Opening his mouth, Ivan gestured to it. *"Otch ote?"*

"What?" Aaron glanced at his hip. "Oh. Stole it from a bandit who tried to kill me in my sleep."

"Hm." Ivan gave him a short once-over. *"It onsazhu shidalgiv."*

Aaron flicked his eyebrows. "Yeah, well, most wouldn't look too great after what I went through. Secret recon mission in the Empire, remember?"

Ivan huffed good-naturedly. "Aaron. You and I both know you would have gone either way. Is why I figured, I might as well give you permission." He shrugged.

The sides of Aaron's mouth jumped into an arrogant smile. *"Uvagalop otch Brent yabet lavonver."*

"Bah, no, Brent was not jealous." Ivan rolled up the map and tucked it into a slot beneath the table, denying Aaron's speculation. Leaning his hands on top of the furniture piece, he bobbed his bearded chin thoughtfully. "Actually…he was."

Aaron's teeth glinted.

"But, he was good about not telling anyone where you went." Ivan waved a hand to brush the matter aside. "But, is enough of that. I will hear your report. Did you learn anything about the scouts, or why they have not been contacting us?"

"I went through Gilead, Ribbosheth, and Devon, but what I heard from our supporters was the same," Aaron replied, all humor leaving him. "The scouts've been missing for at least three weeks by now, give or take a few days. I would've gone further north to find out more but, from what I heard while I was in Devon, I wouldn't have been able to travel much further anyway."

"What do you mean?" A line appeared between Ivan's bushy eyebrows.

"Orinn is walled off."

"Otch?" Clearly, Ivan hadn't been expecting such news. *"Mechaz?"*

"It was attacked, and almost burnt to the ground." Coming forward, Aaron reached for something that was tucked into the back of his belt. Upon its liberation, he spread it out on the table: it was a wanted poster. "Rumor has it that this is the guy who did it."

Ivan's expression was nearly impossible for Aaron to define. But there was no denying the tensing of his features.

The face that stared up from the parchment was disturbing, to say the least. It was most certainly that of someone wearing a mask, one painted black with a devilish grin of sharp teeth and black eyes, as well as a feral mane of hair. But what caught Ivan's eye the most was the symbol on their forehead: it was a circular logo that was made up of interconnecting rings on one half, while those on the other were fractured.

"They're calling him Saruke's Shade," Aaron continued, his careful eyes pinned to Ivan, who was still staring at the etching. When the chief didn't respond, he went on. "You recognize it, don't you? That symbol on his forehead. It looks like the Liberation Fronts' insignia."

Ivan didn't speak.

"From what I heard in Devon, this guy's been causing trouble in Nassaul for about a year." Aaron's straight, upward eyebrows slanted even further. "But what I don't understand is why none of us have heard so much as a sneeze about him until now."

"Where did you find this?" Ivan asked at last, indicating the notice.

"I ran into a group of soldiers on the royal highway. They were keeping it for reference, so, I took it when they weren't paying attention." Aaron breezed over the theft as if it wasn't important. "They mentioned something, though: the imperial government hasn't released official news about this guy so it doesn't cause a panic. Which kinda suggests that whoever he is, they think he's a bigger threat than we are. But the brand on his mask, and his name… Saruke's Shade."

It hadn't taken him very long to remember where he'd first heard the title. Or rather, something that had sounded close to it.

"'Çaru'qu doesn't make mistakes'," he quoted evenly.

Remembrance glinted in Ivan's bright eyes.

"Why does Saruke's Shade share our insignia?" Aaron held the chief's gaze emphatically. "Do you think he's connected to that masked guy Brent and Liam saw in Lenora?"

Ivan didn't respond with words, at least not at first. There was a low grumbling in the deepest parts of his throat, as if he was contemplating the best way to answer Aaron's pointed inquiries.

"I do…recognize this mask," he started at length, looking over the poster. "But, it has been years since I last saw it. Is from before you were born. I doubt if person wearing it now is same as who it was given to."

"And who was that?"

"…An old friend." Ivan straightened and he cleared his throat. "Is…no longer with us. So whoever this 'Shade' is…I do not believe it is same person I know."

"In that case," Aaron continued evenly, "any ideas as to why the imperials nicknamed him Saruke's Shade?"

"I do not know why this would be," the chief answered with a complimentary shake of his head. "Legends say Çaru'qu would appear to his foes as terrifying black lion, or as dicanus. Or…" He searched for the right Arkanian word to use, but it came out in Katruskan, *"Nizhyuf,* of both."

"Fusion?" Aaron echoed, almost skeptic.

Ivan nodded. *"Ahd.* From what I understand of mask, the first owner had it designed with this in mind. Perhaps there is someone else in Empire who knows this story and made up the title, which has stuck."

His straight face hinted at the authenticity of his admission. So, Aaron saw no reason to question him any further.

Still with his eyes lowering, he frowned and folded his arms. "I just wanna know who we can trust and who we can't. Especially since we've got more trouble on the way."

"Explain."

"Empyrean's Guard is suspicious of Odelwhite Forest." Aaron unfolded his arms. "There's a chance they think it's our hideout, and they might stage an attack soon. And it won't be the kind that our aetheriests have been able to stave off for all these years. They've got their hands on some kind of elixir," he elaborated carefully. "Something that increases their quintessence. I got compromised so

I wasn't able to figure out all the details. But from what I did learn, if we're not careful, Taranis could end up like all the sister villages we've lost."

Ivan's expression became just as morbid as his son's. His brow furrowed and twisted, and a shadow descended upon his normally glowing eyes.

"There's…one more thing." Aaron's eyebrows, though still crinkled behind his messy fringe, arched with a touch of sadness. "While I was in Devon, I had a run-in with some bounty hunters and soldiers."

Ivan grunted. *"Tishuran."*

"Ahd. Thomas helped me escape, and the tunnel he had me use brought me outside of town, into the ruins of a supporter's house just out in the fields."

Ivan looked up slowly, thinking, reading between the lines of Aaron's words. His heart sank. "Ruins?"

"Adelle…her last name was Lecil, wasn't it?" Aaron asked. "Did she have a relative who lived not too far from her?"

"Yes," Ivan replied hollowly. "Her cousin."

"Oh…" Aaron was quiet for a second. "Well…their house is a heaping pile of ashes now. From the sign that was hammered into the front yard, it looks like it happened three years ago."

Ivan's eyebrows rose, and for a second Aaron thought that his eyes had moistened.

When the great giant of a man finally spoke, he sounded a little hoarse. "Three years?"

"Yeah." Aaron nodded and a painful pause stretched between them. "I…remember that you and Mom were close to their family." He shifted. "D'you remember the cousin's name?"

"…Lemmiere." Ivan's eyes wandered away and became distant. "Although…" He huffed out a short and bitter laugh. "He liked to be called Lemm." His face fell. "So…he has been captured. And traded into slave system."

"Lemm," Aaron repeated, though the name brought no memories to his mind. He looked at his father. "I'm sorry."

Ivan nodded distractedly. "Is that all?"

"Yes, sir."

"Good. Thank you for your report. Be on standby for further orders."

Aaron bobbed his chin simply, silently.

"You are dismissed."

Aaron nodded again, and without another word he headed for the door.

"And Aaron," Ivan called.

Aaron turned questioningly.

"Do not speak of what you learned to anyone," the chief commanded. His gaze was hard, and seemed to pin Aaron in place. "Understand?"

Aaron hesitated, looking like he wanted to say something. But, choosing against it, he bowed his chin once more. "Sir."

A moment after Aaron had departed, Ivan's eyes fell to the wanted poster that was still laying in front of him. Reaching out, he picked it up.

He had so many questions. But unlike with Aaron, there was no one for him to pose them to.

"Yeah? So you think you're an aetheriest, huh?" Kro crossed his arms with an amused but disbelieving smile.

While admittedly not Mekial's first choice when it came to seeking out advice, Kro was the only aetheriest who was currently available to help him solve his dilemma. Trickles of people ambled around them as they conversed, with younger children scurrying at their heels, and at the edge of the main road an elderly Avat scolded a pair of teens for nearly knocking her over while they'd been running.

Undeterred by the level of activity that surrounded them, Mekial kept his attention on Kro and shrugged in the face of his doubts — doubts that he himself hadn't overcome. "Well, I mean… maybe I am," he said. "I dunno."

"Well, I've got news for you, runt." Dropping his hands to his hips Kro circled around Mekial as if he meant to walk away. Of course, he didn't. *"Being* an aetheriest and thinking you *might* be an aetheriest are two totally different things. You either are one, or you're not." He looked at the boy over his shoulder. "Sure, there are some lucky guys out there that are innate, but people like that hardly pop up these days. So if you wanna learn, it's not gonna be easy."

Mekial's eyebrows furrowed with distaste. "If you're trying to scare me out of it, it's not working."

"Oh? So you wanna learn from me then, is that it?" Kro faced him, smug. "News of me being Taranis' best aetheriest has finally been getting around. I am a bit of a jack-of-all-trades after all."

"Actually, I wanted to ask Heldar," Mekial confessed thoughtfully. "But I hear he's busy right now."

Kro felt like he'd been punched in the gut.

"Then I was gonna ask Tyre, but I couldn't find him," Mekial continued. "Maybe he went with Liam."

Kro felt like he got gut-punched again.

"So, I guess you'll do," Mekial finished.

Kro recovered with a forced smile. "So glad I could be your last resort."

"Yeah. You're welcome."

Kro's smile tightened and he withheld his desire to quip back. After all, Mekial was Renée's brother.

Maybe this'd earn him some brownie points.

"Well, this 'last resort's' actually got a lot of wisdom to share, believe it or not," he said. "And when it comes to deciding if you really wanna train to become an aetheriest, I can tell you that there's only one way to find out."

"Okay…" Mekial couldn't help but feel a bit unsettled by Kro's cunning expression.

But he wanted to become an aetheriest. Or at least, discover if he was one already.

He steeled himself. "What is it?"

Kro smiled impishly.

When the door to Greta's hut clicked open, Lilian's head popped up and out of her tasseled blanket.

It was after dark and, according to Greta, way past her bedtime. Squinting through the shadows that hung over the one-room hut, she peered over her collection of colorful pillows and handmade stuffed animals to see who'd walked inside.

Judging by the silhouette, it was her uncle.

He shut the door quietly, shielding the hut from the crisp night air, and he crossed to the other side of the room to remove his weapons.

Lilian lifted her small face, freeing her mouth from her blanket. "Uncle Liam?"

He stopped in the middle of placing his sword on his weapons rack. Then, he continued to disarm himself. "You should be asleep, Lil."

"I know, but…I wanted to wait until you got back."

Hanging up the belt for his sword last, Liam turned and crossed the room towards her.

The curtains that were blocking the windows were drawn back, allowing soft moonbeams to filter in and land on Greta, who was already resting on her sleeping mat by the fireplace. She was surrounded by a collection of containers that held jewelry making supplies, as well as colorful stones that were likely going to be assembled into accessories for the villagers. Judging by the level of her breathing, she'd fallen asleep long before Liam had gotten home.

The light also fell on the low shelves of dishes and clothing that were pressed against the opposite wall, as well as the equally short dining table that was in the middle of the room. The cushions that served as its seats were still encircling it, their plush faces a strong temptation, and all across the earthen floor tasseled rugs embroidered with delicate designs lay to absorb Liam's steps.

"I'm back," he said to his niece. Moving to the far side of the hut, which was where her sleeping area was, he grabbed the edge of a straw room divider, meaning to wall off her space and the space that was designated as the closest thing he'd ever have to a room. "Now go to sleep."

"Wait!" The little girl sat up quickly, making her stuffed animals roll to the ground. Reaching over, she switched on an oil lamp that had been sitting next to her head and held up a small object for him to see.

He squinted, then knelt to get a better look.

It was a small musical instrument, built against the flat half of a wooden shell. Staggered metal tines were attached to it and a beautiful, hand-painted image was visible on the wooden board beneath them.

"Is that…?" He sat down and took it from her gently.

"Grandma said that it used to be Mom's," Lilian began. "She said it's called a qa…" She frowned. "A qa…"

"Qalimba." Liam didn't look up from it.

"Yeah. That." Lilian crossed her legs beneath her blanket as Liam looked the instrument over, his eyes veiled behind his thoughts. "Grandma said you and Mom used to play it a lot. When you first came to Taranis. One of the elders gave it to you."

"Where'd you find it?" Liam finally looked at her, his silver eyes even whiter in the firelight.

"Grandma found it today while we were cleaning, after you guys all left. She said she thought she lost it after…well…" She trailed off, her brow puckering sadly.

Liam looked back at the qalimba, then over his shoulder.

Greta was still sleeping soundly.

After his sister had passed away, he hadn't wanted anything more to do with the musical tool. He remembered the day clearly: without regard for the story behind it — how it'd been passed down from parent to child until it'd reached the hands of a village elder, who'd then given it to Laura — he'd thrown it across the room, hoping it would break apart.

It hadn't.

It was a wonder Greta had kept it at all. He supposed he'd have to ask her about that later, when time permitted.

"Can I hear you play it?" Lilian begged, drawing Liam's eye again. "Please?"

He looked at the instrument and stroked one of its tines with the edge of his thumb. "…You were thinking about this all day, weren't you?"

Lilian nodded urgently.

Liam looked at her and saw the eagerness in her dark eyes. If he knew anything about this little girl, it was that she would hound him about this new discovery until he caved in. Not even he had the strength to withstand her persistence.

He sighed. "C'mon," he said and he got to his feet. "We'll play it outside, so we don't wake Grandma."

Lilian grinned excitedly and leaped to her feet.

"Get your shoes."

"Okay!"

"Keep your voice down."

"Okay," she whispered, giggling.

The village was quiet when they stepped out, and the roads were empty. But if Liam listened carefully he could catch the sound of the night watch patrolling the paths, and an upward glance in this direction or that would allow him to see the furred edges of their torchlights circling corners or blinking between homes.

Lilian in tow, he went away from the lights and came to the side of Greta's hut. There, a ladder leaned against the side of the little abode.

Qalimba in hand, Lilian excitedly climbed it first.

Liam went after her. Without even looking, he calmly snatched the girl a split second before she could topple off the roof. She herself barely seemed to realize how close she'd come to falling.

Pulling her into his lap, he held his hands out for her to put the qalimba into them, which she did.

"It's been a while," he warned. "Don't know if I remember how to do it."

"I trust you, Uncle," Lilian said, twisting her head around to cast him an adorable smile.

The smile that he gave in response was smaller than hers, a simple curling of closed lips. Setting his eyes on the musical instrument that sat in his palms, he stroked the tines with his thumbs.

Scratching one, he flicked his finger against it.

A melodic chime rang out, echoing over the hut's rooftop to sing into the whispering night.

Lilian waited.

Liam took a second to gather to himself the memories that that one sound had called, memories of a time that suddenly felt much closer than it ever had been: the days where his sister had still been alive, strolling along the roads of Taranis alongside him or her friends; the days where Lilian was still developing in her mother's womb; the days where things seemed to have taken a turn for the better for the both of them — the days where Taranis was fresh and new and when, for the first time in years, they'd been able to relax in a bosom of rest and serenity.

Peace.

And quiet.

Safety.

And hope.

And he remembered.

He struck another tine and left the note to ripple out over the farmlands, into the grasslands, beyond the sprinkling of trees and over the heads of wandering night critters.

He struck another note after that, then a chord. Then delicately, he transitioned into a lullaby that Laura herself had written and had often played over her womb in preparation of the day when her daughter would finally be able to hear it on this side of life.

All that had been before…during a time that, with this instrument as his link, he had clear access to. As if the melody that he now thumbed into this instrument could bridge the gap that existed between now and then, and guide his niece into those days with him.

He lost himself in it — in that flow, that transcendence. And even after Lilian had drifted off to sleep in his arms he continued to play, his notes accompanied by the sigh of the night and the gentle cry of crickets lost in a sea of grass.

He wished the bridges could actually connect.

Even if it was just once.

57

M Y, MY…LOOKS LIKE *you've been forced a terrible hand, haven't you?"*

Brent, his tunic soiled and his sandaled feet covered in the grime of the sewers, lifted his weary head.

Beyond the overpass that he'd found shelter under, a soft rain was falling from the overcast sky, pattering against the cobbled backstreets and sighing across the air. It made the whole city gloomy and bleak, edging his sight with shades of gray that blended into a veil of mist. The only color that interrupted it came from the strands of blue hair that hung into his eyes.

He blinked tiredly, and suddenly became aware of the fact that his head felt heavy. A split second of thought reminded him that it was because he was still wearing his golden, laurel wreath crown.

With foggy eyes, he searched for the person who'd spoken to him.

It was a man, and he towered over Brent like a dark shadow. Long, black hair fell about midway down his back, and he was resting one hand atop the tattered hat that sat on his head.

When he smiled, it was unpleasant.

Brent's expression hardly changed. He only continued to look up with those tired, empty eyes, as if he'd lost the will to feel anything.

And, in fact, after all that he'd experienced the previous night, he had.

"You're going to need a change of clothes if you want to survive out here, chouja," the man told him.

Brent looked down listlessly.

His tunic, hemmed with crimson and gold, was soiled and splattered with blood that wasn't his; his sandals, embroidered with gold filigree, were ripped and falling apart in some places; his golden armlets were stained with mud of a curious odor; the deep blue sash that wrapped around his body was torn and looked as if it'd been dipped in ink.

"Tsk, tsk…"

Still moving at that same dazed pace, Brent looked at the Avat once more.

Renthor smiled strangely.

"It doesn't feel real, does it?"

Brent's eyes flew open.

Laying flat on his back in bed, he stared at the ceiling of his room and beyond — to the roof over his head.

He blinked.

⚬ ✣ ⚬

As dawn's pale, early light crept over the horizon, Mekial stood at the easternmost reaches of the valley and frowned at the wall of trees and shrubs before him, their tangled mess of branches creating a barrier that not even a squirrel could fit through. His little cloak fluttered over his brightly colored village clothes, providing little disguise for the world that existed beyond this forested wall, and his short hair shifted along with it.

Behind him, Dillon, Klarys, Kurt and Lacey craned their necks to see how high the wall of plants went. It seemed to touch the clouds.

They were dressed similarly to him: no stash of imperial disguises in the Main House were small enough for them, so they'd opted to wear cowls over their village clothes. Those with Avat blood had tied strips of fabric around their heads to cover their ears.

Truth be told, rather than appear like a group of imperial children, as was their intent, they looked more like a band of orphaned misfits.

Lacey looked over her shoulder.

Taranis was a distant cluster of houses in the wide scape of pasture behind them, neatly settled atop a grassy mount at the edge of a wall of thick, dark pines. Gentle sunbeams crowned it, and tiny villagers paced the roads.

She wondered if any of them would notice that she and her friends were gone.

All at once, a certain speck of movement caught her eye, and her ears shivered at the sound of rustling in the grass. She squinted for a moment, then realized that a small person was running towards them.

Her heart clenched, thinking they'd been found out, but a split second later the little girl's face was revealed.

Lacey's mouth fell open. "Lilian?!" she exclaimed, and her friends turned around.

"You forgot me!" Lilian cried, slowing to a stop in front of them. As the absolute youngest of the party as well as the smallest, she was practically swimming in the tattered shawl that she was wearing.

It made sense — it was Liam's, after all. So was the close-fitting, seamed hat that she was wearing, which came down to her eyebrows but hid her pointy ears quite well.

The older children exchanged troubled, bothered looks.

Lilian's heart sank. "You…didn't forget me."

"It's dangerous in the Empire, Lil," Dillon said consolingly. "We didn't want to bring you along because you're still a kid."

"*You're* still a kid!" Lilian retorted angrily. "I wanna find out if Mekial's an aetheriest, too! That's not fair!"

Dillon sighed. "You should go back."

"If you make me go back, I'll tell on you! I'll tell Uncle Liam!"

Again the older children looked at one another.

Kurt heaved a sigh and shrugged.

"Just let her come," Mekial said. "If Liam finds out, Ren'll find out, and then Mom'll find out, and then I'll *really* be in trouble."

"Fine." Dillon refaced the newest addition to the party. "But you can't go wandering off anywhere, okay?"

Lilian just cheered and threw her arms into the sky.

Turning back around, Mekial studied the floor of the tangled wall. Then, he dropped to the ground and pressed his cheek against the grass. Straining his eyes in the dimness, his dark gaze scrolled to a narrow tunnel at the bottom of the barrier.

Its walls were made of the same brambles that made up the entire wall and a layer of grass dotted with dandelion seeds spanned its length. It was short and tight, but if he crushed his shoulders in and moved on his belly, he could make it to the other side.

He grinned. "It's really here…I found it!" Leaping to his feet, he turned on his friends. "C'mon, he's waiting for us! We gotta hurry!"

As the mid-afternoon sun reigned with every ounce of its summery strength, Aaron nonchalantly leaned against the outer wall of the sparring hall. With a block of partially sculpted wood in one hand and a small knife in the other, he began to carve it into a shape known only to his hands.

He didn't look up from his work when he spoke. "You good, man?"

"Peachy." Although Brent responded, he didn't look at him. Instead he continued to whirl and arc his staff, practicing his many forms and techniques in the sunny area outside of the designated training space.

"Hmph. Sounds like the rest of us." Aaron tilted his tiny sculpture to get a better look at it and gain a better idea of what he wanted to whittle it into. Coming to a decision, he proceeded to make it a reality. "It's been about a week since I got back, and there's still no word from the scouts…can't say I'm really one for Dad's whole 'wait and see' approach. The scouts are trained to handle themselves in the Empire but if they can't…" His eyes seemed to dim a little. "Well…we all know what happens next." He flicked a shred of wood at the ground and kept carving. "Can't say I like the thought."

"I'm surprised you haven't snuck off all over again." Brent stopped in mid-swing, holding his stance. Transitioning into a new pose, he continued his routine. "Aaron son of Ivan, top recon scout and leader of runaways. You could probably form your own special unit.

"But you're right. It's been at least a month now." Brent spun his staff into a resting position. His downcast eyes were shadowed with thought. "I'm getting restless. At this rate, I don't think Pops is even thinking to send out a retrieval team. But I did ask him about it."

"Yeah. I overheard you guys this morning." Aaron shaved off another piece of wood as he alluded to the earlier conversation. His next words were oozing with sarcasm. "Sounded like it went great."

Brent scoffed. "I also tried looking into that stuff about the Shades, and Zion again. But the only info I could gather was from the schoolhouse plays. I even went through the Main House archives the other day but there was nothing there, either."

"Probably means that Dad and the others take this deal that they made with the Elder that seriously." Aaron shaved off another piece of wood. "Same thing about the 'Shades' that the councilman mentioned. Which begs the question: if the Shades are s'posed to stay out of sight, why are they letting us see them?"

Brent paused. "…Maybe we're not supposed to."

"What?"

"The guy that Xëri spoke to at the Feast." Brent looked at him and then away as he thought it over. "He was invisible at first. But somehow I could still tell that he was there." He looked at Aaron again, who was now watching him with a skeptical look on his face. "What if that other guy I keep seeing is the same? What if I'm not really…*supposed* to being seeing him at all?"

"Well, if the Shades are aetheriests, then making themselves invisible isn't that crazy of an idea." Aaron went back to whittling. "Don't know what to make of this man of your dreams, though."

Brent just looked at him, annoyed. "Whoever he is, I can't figure out what he wants. As for the Shades, they obviously enjoy keeping their secrets. And talking in riddles," he added crossly, for he still hadn't deciphered what the Shade back in Lenora had told him: the howl of a "coming storm" and a threat that was worse than the imperial slave trade looming in the Empire. He'd also mentioned someone or something named Çaru'qu — Brent still had no leads on that whatsoever. "Same as Pops and Xëri." Turning away, he went back to training. "So, until I can make more sense of it, I figured I should focus on the problems that we've got going on right now. Like how we haven't gone on a raid in over a month because our intel scouts have gone dark."

"And that's why you tried to talk Dad into sending a retrieval team. Led by you."

"We can't just abandon them." Brent spun his staff in a figure eight around his body. "Even with all this other stuff going on…" He settled into a new resting stance. "They're still important. Pops has to see that."

"…Y'know," Aaron straightened up against the wall of the sparring hall and finally turned his complete focus onto Brent, "you may be the village's best strategist, but you're not part of the head council."

Brent circled and eyed him challengingly. "What?"

"You heard me." Aaron pushed off the wall. "Dad's as stubborn as they come. Even you know that. And you're just a raider. He won't listen to you."

Brent held silent for a second, weighing whether or not he should try to find a fault in Aaron's statement. In the end he decided not to and resumed his training session.

"But you're the one who's right this time." Aaron's scowl dissipated only a little. "If you want results, you're better off sneaking out of Taranis and looking for the scouts yourself."

Startled by his frank statement, Brent rounded on him.

"What?" Aaron raised a deadpan eyebrow. "You think I'm kidding?"

Brent didn't. But he searched Aaron's face anyway.

There wasn't even the faintest hint of jest.

"You're not the only one who's worried about the scouts," Aaron continued seriously. "All of us are." He paused and his bright gaze fell. "…I think we might've been spoiled this past year."

The sides of Brent's eyes tightened in curious confusion.

"How?"

"Things have been going pretty well since you started raiding," Aaron said, looking at him. "As far as our forces are concerned, there haven't been any casualties and none of us have been recaptured. But with how the scouts have been acting, there's a chance that the slave traders have switched things up again. It happens, and it means we'll have to adjust. Just like we always do. After that," the shadows on his face receded a bit, "we can get back to showing those imperials who they're messing with. For the sake of every slave, and every one of us that they've ever taken."

Brent nodded, grateful for Aaron's like-mindedness.

"Things might get a little tricky, though," the redhead continued. "Dad plans to send a new team of intel scouts out tomorrow."

"What? Since when?"

"Since yesterday." Aaron's face was calm in a grim sort of way. "Liam told me. He's supposed to be part of that rotation so, naturally, you and I are gonna be expected to stay in Taranis until he sends in a report."

Brent's golden eyes fell, his thoughts speeding a mile a minute.

Aaron stepped away from the sparring hall and into the sunlight. "Intel scouts usually trickle out of the valley over the course of the night but if we try to leave with Liam outright, Dad'll definitely stop us."

Brent slipped into Aaron's train of thought. "So we leave on our own. Probably the night after at the earliest."

"Or two, to be safe," Aaron countered. "But then there's the matter of having someone cover for us. I may not always agree with my old man, but he's still the chief. If word gets out that I keep sneaking off without his leave, it could cause trouble for him with everybody else. Especially the newer villagers. Both of his sons being gone'll be even more bothersome…"

Brent couldn't hold in his laughter. "So the runaway's got a guilty conscience after all."

Aaron wasn't amused. "…There's one more thing," he added, returning to his sculpture. He cut off a few sharp corners, shaving it into the shape of an entelodon. "Dad wanted me to keep it a secret, but I figured you oughta know since it kind of involves you:

I might have a lead on that Çaru'qu thing."

"Seriously?" Brent's narrow eyes got big. "Found somethin' while you were away?"

"Yeah," Aaron confirmed and his ears shivered at the sound of someone running at him from behind. He didn't bother turning to see who it was. After all, he could already tell who the footsteps belonged to. "I'll tell you in a bit."

"Right," Brent agreed, having also heard the approaching villager.

White hair flashed over Aaron's shoulder.

"Hi, Eklaire," he said without looking up.

"Arghh!" Eklaire skidded to a stop behind him, her head flying back as she shook her fists. "Aaron!" She stomped her foot. "You always ruin it!"

"It's not my fault I can hear you coming from a mile away!" he retorted as she circled to stand in front of him. He looked at her. "You're terrible at being sneaky! We're lucky you're not a scout."

Eklaire blew air out of her mouth hard enough to make her lips roll.

Aaron's eyes darted to the basket that was strapped to her back. "Are you going somewhere?"

"As a matter of fact, I was just on my way out!" She nodded proudly and turned to catch sight of Brent. "What're ya'll doin'? Trainin'?"

"…Yeah." Brent twirled his staff and started another round of sequential moves. "It's been a pretty slow month."

"Ohhh…" Eklaire's mouth formed a little circle as she nodded. "Well then," she brightened up, "I've got the perfect thing fer ya'll to do to get rid of yer boredom!"

"Yeah?" Aaron raised an eyebrow. "What's that?"

"This!" Beaming, Eklaire whipped a piece of parchment out of her waist sash and held it out to him.

Putting his knife and wood carving into one hand, he took it. "What's this?"

"Ya'll are gonna help me go prune pickin'!" Spinning around, she wiggled her basket at him excitedly.

"What?" He looked up confusedly and a split second later, his eyebrows slanted in denial. "No way!"

"Yes way!" Eklaire jumped, circling in midair so she could face him when she landed. "The chief said that the raiders who take my request are gonna be my bodyguards!"

"We didn't take any request!"

"What's that you took right there?" Eklaire tilted her head a little, her eyes twinkling as she leaned towards him.

Aaron glanced at the note and back at her.

Brent moved closer to get a better look.

Aaron's eyes returned to the piece of parchment. With a frown, he unfolded it.

It was a commission for a non-imperial assignment, made official thanks to what he instantly recognized as his father's signature on the left-hand side. He read the Arkanian script swiftly, following it from top to bottom, right to left.

Plainly, it said,

Escort Request to: Arkanian Prune Plateau
Made by: Eklaire Dunbar

In the space below Ivan's signature, there was another spot where the raider — or raiders — who agreed to escort Eklaire could write in their names, thus signing to take on her request.

But Aaron's and Brent's names were already there.

In Eklaire's handwriting.

Aaron's eyebrow twitched. "You little…"

Eklaire giggled. "Thanks fer the help, Aaron!"

Brent took the notice from him.

"It's legit," Aaron admitted as he studied it.

"You already wrote our names in?" Brent looked at Eklaire.

"Mm-hmm!" She nodded. "It'll be fun! Plus, I ain't seen ya'll in a while!"

"You saw us yesterday." Aaron squinted at her.

"But that was just in passin'! That don't count! 'Sides, yesterday was like…a whole day ago!" She flipped her arms up and dropped them to her sides.

Aaron smirked. "What, can't stand to be apart from us for that long?"

"Guess we make an impression," Brent joined.

"Oh, don't give yerselves so much credit! It ain't like I'm part of yer fan club." Eklaire snatched the note back. "I actually just wrote yer names in while I was on my way over here. It ain't like I didn't see ya'll's faces when you started talkin'. Didn't seem like much of a happy chat."

Brent and Aaron exchanged looks.

"So," Aaron pieced the meaning of Eklaire's words together, "this is your attempt at cheering us up?"

"Ya'll just need a lil' change of scenery!" Eklaire grinned, her hands on her hips. "Things ain't really been all that happy 'round here at all, what with them scouts ain't comin' back, even though they shoulda been. It's got everybody down in the dumps. I woulda put Ren'n Liam down too, but Liam's busy fixin' a hole in Greta's roof'n Ren's already taken on so many requests that she's busier than a one-legged man in a butt-kickin' contest!"

"And we're not busy?"

"Please, you were cuttin' wood while Brent was swingin' a stick."

"I'm carving!"

"It's a bladed staff!" Brent corrected at the same time, holding it out. He pulled back when Eklaire suddenly thrust the folded note into his face.

"Anyway, I'm gonna go ahead'n drop this off at the Main House so the chief'll know where ya'll are!" Her face was bright. "You know, in case of an emergency or somethin'."

"Oh, how thoughtful," Aaron said flatly.

"Oh, don't be such a sour prune! We're gonna have so much *fun!*" Eklaire thrust her fist into the air. "To the plateauuuu!" she cheered, and she ran around the sparring hall to reach the shortcut to the Main House.

Brent and Aaron watched her go in silence.

"Um…" Brent planted the end of his staff into the ground again, partly surprised by how quickly Eklaire had changed the course of their day. Then again, she had a knack for doing that. "To the…plateau…then…"

Aaron sighed.[tv]

A LEAD AT LAST
CODE: THESHADE

58

HEARING A RUSTLING in the bushes at his back, Kro turned from the river in Odelwhite Forest with a gleam in his eye. As he expected, Mekial was coming into view. "Well! Look who finally decided to show…up…"

Mekial's friends trailed into the clearing next.

Kro's shoulders dropped, as did his jaw.

"I'm here!" Mekial bounded into the sunshine with an eager grin. "Made it here just after daybreak, like we agreed."

Kro just face-palmed. Loudly.

He wasn't wearing his jewelry and sleeveless tabard, nor the loose pants banded at the ankle that were common to his village outfit. Instead he'd opted for an imperial look, one that was far more convincing than what the children were wearing. But, similar to his everyday attire, his hard arms were visible thanks to his sleeveless, belted tunic.

"I thought we agreed that it'd just be me and you," he reminded Mekial and he looked at the other children. "I'm not Yulia, this isn't a class field trip!"

"We'll be quiet!" Dillon promised. Though he was clearly trying to advocate for himself and his friends, their lineup of absent or distracted expressions did little to help his case. Lilian even started picking her nose. "You won't even know we're here. Promise!"

"Stop that," Klarys chided, pulling Lilian's finger out of her face.

"I just wanted to see Mekial do cool aether stuff!" Lilian cried, holding up a hand to speak like she was in a classroom setting. Liam's ragged shawl started sliding off of her shoulder and his hat slipped into her eyes. She moved to fix both.

"You don't need to raise your hand —" Kro started before he face-palmed again. "Wait what am I saying? You brought Liam's niece with you?!" He rounded on Mekial. "He'll rip me in half when he finds out!"

"Technically she came on her own," Klarys pointed out, adjusting Lilian's hat for her.

"Nuance."

"I won't tell Uncle!"

"What's a 'nuance'?" Kurt cocked his head.

"Ugh, fine, whatever. Look." Kro rubbed his forehead and looked at Mekial, one gloved fist sitting on his hip. "I agreed to help you figure out if you're an aetheriest. But when we get back to Taranis, you're taking the fall for bringing your friends along."

"Sure." Mekial grinned. "Right after you take the fall for telling a bunch of kids to leave the valley."

Kro furrowed his brow. "Do you want my help, or not? Cuz I could easily bring you all back to Taranis now and say you wandered off alone. Who d'you think they'll believe: me, the border scout currently on patrol, or the kids dressed up like a bunch of runaways?"

Mekial and his friends exchanged looks.

They all knew that venturing outside of Taranis was forbidden to anyone who wasn't an auction raider or a scout. It was why getting from the valley and into Odelwhite was a nigh-impossible feat unless you were going on a mission, in which case an aetheriest would join you and force the wall of forestry out of your way.

Mekial was also aware of the fact that Odelwhite was in the southwestern-most region of the Province of Lyrik, the nearest territory of the Arkanian Empire. Additionally, he knew that going to such a place with his friends was something only a fool would do, especially since his friends weren't trained to defend themselves.

But evidently, he'd ventured out here and had allowed his friends to come along.

While their company hadn't been something that he'd been planning on, he knew one thing for sure: he had to meet with Kro and go to Revere Falls, a magnificent grouping of waterfalls that existed within the rich greenery of Odelwhite. If he didn't, he wasn't sure if he'd ever find out if what had happened with the entelodon had been something aetherial, or if it'd just been a fluke.

At least, that's what Kro had told him.

So he couldn't go back. He wouldn't — even if it meant getting in trouble later.

"Okay, okay." He faced Kro soberly. "I won't tell anyone."

Kro eyed him for a second and he cast the others a short, thoughtful glance.

They all looked disappointed.

He sighed in defeat. "All right…after we're done, I'll show you guys how to get back to Taranis without me and without getting caught. That way you'll be in the clear, too. Would've been easier to handle if I only had one kid to worry about but, whatever."

The children exchanged grins.

"All right. Ready to go?" Kro jabbed a thumb upstream. "The falls are this way."

"Ready!" Lilian cried, and she raced along the riverbank, arms spread like she was flying.

"Wait up, Lil!" Kurt called, going after her. "Don't run off!"

"Hey!" Dillon and Mekial chased them.

"Wait for me!" Lacey wailed, hustling to catch up.

Klarys and Kro followed at a walking pace.

"So, are you like, the down-to-earth one?" he asked her.

Klarys passed him a look. Then, she ran ahead to join the others.

He sighed. "What have I gotten myself into…"

✢

The grove that the Arkanian prunes grew in was a tiny area, settled atop a plateau in the valley beyond the amari tree. It consisted of short trees with thin, leafy branches, and thanks to how they were scattered across the flat terrain they gave the place a peaceable appearance. The severe lack of undergrowth only enhanced this.

Its quaint look couldn't be taken for granted however, for the area was located a fair distance from Taranis. Any careless individual who stopped to peruse the trees could unwittingly cross paths with a dangerous, and likely hungry, animal at any moment.

Fortunately though, the place was quiet on this day. So, Eklaire's hired guard elected to walk through the grove at a calm stride for, while the risk of danger was present, the place was so open that there was ample chance to see when it was coming.

Knowing this and trusting her friends for their protection, Eklaire skipped ever closer to the central clearing, for it was there that the prunes preferred to grow. She hummed as she went and as soon as she reached the clearing, she twirled happily.

When she did, she noticed that Brent and Aaron were talking to one another in hushed voices. Whatever it was they were discussing, it was clear that they didn't want her to listen in.

She frowned.

"And what're you two whisperin' about?" she challenged, hands on her hips.

"Nothin'," Aaron said automatically, finishing whatever he had been whispering to Brent about.

Eklaire clearly didn't believe him. Then, she grinned. "I bet it was girl trouble, huh?"

"What?" Aaron blushed. "No!"

"Then why're you turnin' redder than Hubert's tomatoes at pickin' time?"

"I'm not red!"

"You're so red, dude," Brent sniggered.

"Shut up, whose side are you on?!"

Eklaire giggled. "If ya need some advice with girls, I'm here for ya, Aaron!"

"I don't need your advice," Aaron refuted grumpily, turning aside, and he absently passed his fingers through his hair. "I can handle girls on my own, thanks."

"Whoa, boy, check you out! Does Lady Xëri know that yer a

lady-*killer?!*"

Aaron turned scarlet. "Would you stop?! That's not what I meant!"

"I think yer little hair flip says otherwise!"

Aaron just rubbed his face with a quiet grumbling sound.

"Maybe you should take some of her advice, man," Brent laughed. "You get flustered so easily!"

"I got plenty of advice fer you, too, Brent!" Eklaire added, wheeling on him. "You'n Ren're tearin' my nerves up!"

It was Brent's turn to be embarrassed. "What?! What'd we do?!"

"Pfeh, now who's flustered?" Aaron prodded.

Brent frowned at him, still pink in the face.

Eklaire giggled.

The boys looked at her.

"Glad someone's enjoying themselves," Aaron said.

"Of course I am! Makin' fun of ya'll is just too easy." Eklaire winked. "Plus, we're at the plateau! Where Arkanian prunes are… everywhere!" She threw her arms into the sky and spun around again, giggling. "Ya can't be all glum and serious when there're prunes involved, can ya?"

"Who's being glum?" Aaron scowled.

"Ya'll were!"

"I don't know what you're talking about." He looked away.

Eklaire smiled sarcastically. "Some things just don't change, huh, Aaron?"

He bristled. "What's *that* s'posed to mean?!"

Her mismatched eyes sparkled as she laughed.

At the sight of that, Aaron loosened up a little and his frown melted away. He even blushed a bit.

"Now, let's get to pickin'!" Rounding on the clearing, Eklaire darted into it and began to hunt through the tree leaves for some choice prunes.

Grunting, Aaron turned and started for the plateau's edge.

Brent frowned. "Where're you going?"

"Um." Aaron sent him a strange look. "To keep watch?"

"You're not even gonna help?" Brent jabbed a thumb at Eklaire.

"We can't all have our heads in the trees," Aaron pointed out and he continued along the unmarked path that would guide him back to the lip of the plateau. The valley that lunged away from the amari tree was settled just below it and since any wild animals that would want to attack them — or simply enter the grove — would likely come from there, it was the perfect place to stand guard. "'Sides," he shot a cocky smile over his shoulder, "who best to take down a rampaging entelodon if it shows up?"

Brent didn't answer, though this time it was more out of acknowledgement of what Eklaire had just said.

Some things just didn't change.

Turning back around, Aaron continued on his way.

With a half smile and a soft shake of his head, Brent headed into the clearing.

"Aww, is Aaron too mopey to hang out with us?" Eklaire pretended to pout and projected her voice loudly enough for Aaron to hear her.

Aaron didn't turn. He just folded his arms and leaned against a tree when he reached the grove's edge.

"Decided he'd keep watch." Brent looked at Aaron with her. "He's getting too old to pick prunes anymore, anyway. He might pull something."

"I heard that!" Aaron barked.

Brent and Eklaire cringed.

But when they looked at each other, they laughed.

Eklaire spun to face the clearing again, stretching her arms over her head as she sighed. "I can't believe how long it's been!" She approached one of the trees and deeming its prunes worthy of picking, she took off her basket and stood it in the grass. Reaching up, she plucked two prunes free from the serrated, four-lobed capsules that held them. "The last time I came out here was with Mama back when Ren was graduatin' so we could make some pies fer the Feast. But, it's nice to have new company. Or old." She stuck her tongue out at Brent teasingly when he started to work from a tree near her.

"Hey!" He faked a frown.

She giggled and returned to her work.

Finding a prune that he thought looked particularly tasteful, Brent picked it free. It was of a decent size, having grown to be almost as large as a small apple.

He could still remember the first time he'd ever seen a prune and how he'd curled his lip in uninformed disgust, put off by its blue leaves and red-seeded face. The words of the man who'd held it out to him were still a part of that memory.

"It's an Arkanian prune," he'd said. *"They're good for you. And they're sweet."*

Brent smiled crookedly. Then, glancing at Eklaire, he bounced the dark fruit in his hand. "So…how many of these did you say you needed, again?"

She didn't turn from her picking. "Just enough to fill that basket."

"Oh. Okay." He brought it to his mouth. "Then, I'll just eat this one and grab another after…"

"What? No!" She tried to stop him. "That's a good one! It's all nice'n plump —!"

"You don't want this one!" he laughed, spiraling away before she could snatch it from him. "It'll take up too much room in the basket!"

"No it won't!" She lunged again.

"C'mon, Eklaire, I haven't eaten since breakfast!" He side-stepped her and ran around the tree to get away.

"That's because you were too busy swingin' that stick!" She chased him. "That's yer fault!"

"Ooh…that's cold." Moving swifter than she could, he grabbed the tree's thin trunk and swung around it, ending up behind her.

Right when she spun to see him, he took a noisy bite out of the prune.

"Brent!"

He retreated. "Oh, this one look's pretty good, too!" He grabbed another prune from the highest branches. "Oh, never mind, it's too big. Guess I'll just eat half of it."

"Brent! Quit fiddle-fartin' around'n help me!"

"C'mon, just lemme have a snack! I work harder on a full stomach, anyway!"

"You can eat *after* we're done! *Brent!*"

He laughed.

"Oh…forget it!" Eklaire started picking more prunes from a new tree. "I'll just…get 'em myself…!"

Brent chuckled and wiped his mouth with his arm after finishing his food. "Aw, c'mon, Eklaire! I thought we came out here to get our spirits up. What happened to your sense of fun?"

She slowed at that and although she kept her head pointed at the tree, he could see her smiling.

"Thanks, Brent," she said suddenly, just before he bent down to scoop up her basket.

"What for?" He stepped towards her, bringing the container closer so she wouldn't have to bend down to drop the prunes into it.

Eklaire just shook her head. "Maybe I've just been workin' too much. I always gotta sew clothes, or fix clothes, or help somebody else fix clothes…I think I've just been real uptight lately. And the villagers'n their bein' worried 'bout the scouts ain't been helpin' no-how. Not to say it's their fault or nuthin'. But I just wanted a break'n I think I took it out on ya'll a bit." She twisted her lip and chanced a fast look at him. "D'you…think I was kinda pushy? Y'know, with…makin' ya'll come out here with me?"

Brent's face was blank. "…Yeah."

She grimaced. "Really?"

"Yeah. You were like a tyrant."

"What?!"

"All hail Empress Eklaire! The men of Taranis bow to her every whim" — Brent bowed deeply and looked up with a twinkling eye — "especially when she writes them in for prune picking."

"Prune pickin' is fun!" she protested, shoulders squared. "And I'd make a great empress! I'd put that ol' Koberius to shame!"

"Think you'd have to marry him to get that title."

"Ew, blech! I'd sooner conquer the whole continent'n give him a public execution!"

"Tyrant."

"It'd be justified!"

Brent laughed and with a playful eye-roll, Eklaire plucked another prune free and placed it in the basket along with the rest.

"You were right about one thing though," he went on admittedly, tilting the woven container so the fruits wouldn't stack. "I think we did need to get out of the village for a bit. Least, I did." The side of his mouth curved faintly. "Thanks."

Eklaire caught his eye and after a short second, she smiled in return. Then, she parted the leaves in search of another fruit.

Keeping a steady eye on her, Brent slowly reached into the basket.

Eklaire smacked his hand without looking.

"Ow!"

"Mama's got me trained to have eyes in the back of my head!" she announced proudly.

"What are you, an insect?" he mumbled. *"Ack!"* His head snapped back when she tossed a prune at his head.

It rebounded into the basket.

"Ooh!" Her face lit up. "Did you see that?! Imma do it again!"

"What? No!" He ducked right when she threw another prune at him and it zoomed over his head. He glanced back at it. "Eklaire!"

"Aw, c'mon! Where's yer sense of fun?" She cackled at the look on his face.

⚘

The walk to the source of Odelwhite's river was relaxing, filled with the sound of the children's voices echoing between the trees. The entire wood was calm as they went, untouched by the hands of man so that nature could run freely. It was peaceful and bright, mottled with sunlight and rich with the scent of fresh grass and the low calls of chittering birds. Small creatures sprinted between mossy trees and overgrown stumps; high overhead, the sky was clear and blue. It was almost hard to believe that they were no longer in Taranis' immediate territory. Everything was as tranquil as the valley.

Soon, the howl of the waterfalls rushed through the air, kissing their skin with gentle blasts of mist. Then, after rounding one last towering coast redwood, Revere Falls was revealed in all its glory.

Its rolling torrents bellowed in their ears like thunder, filling the heavens with their sound. There were several falls, rising higher than any of them could crane their necks to see, and they shimmered in the sunlight. Some of them spurted out of the rocky cliffs, others toppled over the crags, and more spilled into others, altogether forming a vivid turbulence that validated the place's name. In some places, they could even see rainbows.

Lilian's eyes grew in amazement. "Wow!"

"It's so pretty!" Klarys exclaimed, her eyebrows raised.

"Whoa…" Kurt joined.

Mekial, Dillon and Lacey simply looked on in soundless wonder.

The river that the falls tumbled into was just as tumultuous, winding past the villagers as rivulets of white. Halfway through it fishes jumped and on the opposite bank, a male doranis drank his fill.

"Look, an arctotherium!" Dillon pointed beyond the bush-antlered buck, to a horned and grizzly creature that was lumbering through the trees behind it. Stout and muscular, it turned its short-eared head and waited.

Seconds later, its furry cub came tottering out of the bushes to join it.

"Wow!" Lilian cried. "This is so cool!"

"And dangerous," Kro added, crossing his arms. "Everyone stay close. Or at least somewhere I can see you."

"Okay!"

"As for you." Kro looked at Mekial and gestured to the riverbank. "Sit down, shut up and listen to me for a sec."

Mekial did so, legs crossed and hands on his ankles.

The others sat around him, eager to hear what Kro had to say.

"The aether is complicated business," he started, dropping to sit in front of them, "so don't go zoning out on me, all right?"

Mekial nodded quickly, as did his friends.

"How much do you actually know about the aether, anyway?"

"Well…" Mekial scratched the side of his chin thoughtfully. "Not too much, honestly."

"Got it." Kro shrugged a shoulder. "Then we'll start with the basics. You guys have to at least know that the aether is made up of something called 'quintessence'."

"Yeah." Dillon nodded. "And that everyone and everything also has quintessence."

"Exactly." Kro pointed at him. "You can think of that as a small deposit of the aether inside of everything."

Dillon nodded his understanding.

"Everyone is born with a small amount of quintessence," Kro continued. "With the proper training, anyone can learn how to draw that energy out and join it with the aether. The more you do that, the more your quintessence grows. The more it grows, the easier it becomes to link with the aether."

"That's how aetheriests use their abilities," Mekial interrupted. "Right? Cuz the aether is connected to everything."

"Yeah, absolutely anything: rocks, sand, plants, trees, air, water, fire…even intangible things like light, pure quintessence, and sound."

"Pure quintessence?" Mekial repeated, frowning.

"I'll get to that." Kro temporarily dismissed the subject with a wave of his hand. "When an aetheriest connects to the aether, they have access to all these things and then some. Their quintessence flows through the aether and into that of another object, where it manipulates it according to the aetheriest's will. That's called influence. So, the more you train, the more your quintessence grows; the more quintessence you have, the stronger your influence."

"Is that why linking to the aether also gets easier?" Kurt asked. "Cuz of influence?"

"Yep."

"Huh." Mekial considered that. "So, when you or Tyre create a windstorm, you're pushing your quintessence against the quintessence of the air through the aether."

"Exactly!" Kro dipped his chin with a proud and attractive smile.

"That's influence."

"Yep."

"Hmm…" Mekial scratched his head. "How does that even work?"

"Influence can be executed with hand motions, but if you've influenced a certain object enough times, connecting to it not only becomes easier, but so does influencing it. Sorta like how you don't need to think too hard about lifting your arm" — he raised his left arm — "it just becomes second-nature."

"Is that why sometimes Tyre can make wind explode around his body without even moving?" Lacey asked.

"Yup. But there are exceptions. Sometimes, even if you're familiar with an element, you still need to move around if you're trying to influence it in a way that you're not used to."

Mekial quirked an eyebrow. "What do you mean?"

"I mean…" Kro's hair and cloak began to shift in a wind that none of them could feel. The motions were gentle, as if he was sitting in a soft, circular breeze.

A moment later something soft touched their cheeks: his quintessence, they realized, expanding out of him to grasp the intangible aether.

In the following second the breeze whispering around his body increased in might, howling around him in wide, arcing circles and knocking the children flat onto their backs, legs akimbo. They grunted audibly.

"This sort of influence doesn't need me to think too much, since I've gotten used to making the wind move in this direction." As he spoke, the gale died. "It's also a natural movement for air, like in storms and stuff, so I don't have to force it to do too much when I use my influence on it."

His small audience sat up weakly.

"But when I'm influencing the air in a way that's unnatural, well, I haven't completely mastered that yet. Neither has Tyre, even though the air is his favorite thing to influence." Kro stood and dusted off his pants. "So, we have to move more."

Spreading his feet into the stance of an aetheriest, he stretched his hands out. He took a breath and then, spinning the wrist of his right hand, he pumped his palm out.

Immediately a spiraling wind erupted from his palm, forcing nearby bushes and branches to lean into its shape as it blasted by.

The children gawked, amazed. "Whoa!"

"Eventually we'll get it." Kro stood upright. "But for now, we are where we are." He looked at the wide-eyed children over his shoulder, and with a cocky smile he turned to face them completely.

"Whoa…" Mekial looked at his hands. "That's cool! And I can do that too?!"

"Well, apparently." Kro gained a curious look. "Didn't you move the barrier to get out here?"

"Huh?" Mekial looked confused for a second. "Oh. No. Actually, I asked Aaron about how he used to sneak out of the valley, and he told me about this little hole in the barrier that he used to crawl through. We came through that."

Kro stared at him.

Then, he smacked his forehead. "I can't believe Grumps actually gave that info up and didn't even ask why you wanted it…"

"He did," Mekial remembered and his eyes shifted away. "He seemed…suspicious. But I just said I was curious."

"You lied?"

"It wasn't a lie!"

A large bubble swelled and popped in the roaring river.

Dillon and Kurt were the only ones who noticed it. The two of them shared a quizzical look.

"Okay, then I guess you failed that test…" Kro ran his fingers through his hair.

"I have a question," Klarys piped up suddenly.

"What?"

"If everyone in the world has quintessence, how come not everyone is an aetheriest?"

"There are certain limitations." Kro crossed his arms. "For example, for Avats."

Dillon, Lacey and Lilian shifted uncomfortably.

Kro felt pity for them for a second. "Despite the different plays put on during the Feast of Liberty every year, Avats can't really connect to the aether. Not sure why — it could be anything, really. The consensus is they're just not born with the same amount of quintessence as Arkanians."

"What's a 'consensus'?" Lilian squinted at him.

"A popular theory."

"What's a theory?"

"A consensus."

"Well then," Lacey, who'd shifted so that one arm was wrapped around her knees, raised her hand before Lilian could argue with him, "how come not all humans are aetheriests?"

"Because not everyone can handle the aether," Kro told her. "It's pure quintessence. Almost everyone has the potential to link to it, but that doesn't change the fact that you're connecting to a power source that literally runs all of existence. A lot of people get overwhelmed when connecting to something like that. It messes with their psyche. Which is why aetheriests need to have a strong mind" — he tapped his temple — "as well as a strong body."

"You mentioned it again," Dillon said. "Pure quintessence. Earlier, you talked about it like it's something you can link to through the aether, like earth or fire."

"Well, when it comes to pure quintessence, there are two types," Kro replied. "One is where you link directly to the aether, which is pretty straightforward. Using the aether in this way lets you do things like create barriers, or hit opponents with pure energy. It's almost like you're influencing the aether itself.

"Then there's excess, which is when an aetheriest links to the aether and then, instead of reaching through it to influence something else, they redirect the aether back at themselves, raising the level of their quintessence and, of course, the power of their influence. Think of it as a temporary power boost."

"Whoa."

"What's *that* look like?!" Kurt exclaimed.

"Yeah, I wanna see!" Lilian cried.

"Same!" Mekial agreed.

"All right…stand back." Kro waved his hands at them, and the children excitedly got to their feet and stood at a safe distance.

Once he had enough room, Kro spread his feet and relaxed his hands by his sides. Again his hair and clothes shifted, and again his quintessence stretched around him, brushing his onlookers.

They watched with bated breath.

Kro inhaled softly. Exhaled.

Then his muscles locked, his knees buckled and the wind gusting around him increased, kicking his cloak into the air and making the children stumble. A supernatural light manifested around his body, starting at his crown and falling to his feet: it was a soft, teal shine that fluttered around him like an aurora.

In seconds, the breeze coursing around him petered out and died. But the light remained.

"Whoa!" The children were amazed.

"This is high excess." Kro watched the stretches of light that were looping around his arm. "If I'd gone with just low excess, the light would been kinda pinkish instead. But this is as far as I'm willing to go when it comes to giving myself a power-up. If I tried raising my quintessence any higher, I wouldn't be able to handle it.

"But again, this is advanced stuff. I doubt Mekial'll get to it today." He looked at the boy and as he spoke he withdrew from the aether, extinguishing the light that hovered around him. "You said that you think you might already be an aetheriest, which'd be impressive since you haven't had any formal training."

"Yeah." Mekial scratched his head. "I guess."

Kro rubbed his mouth, thinking, and his slanted brows drew together. "If that really is the case that'd make you an innate…"

"Wait," Dillon looked from Mekial to Kro, recognizing the term that he'd just used. "You think Mek's a natural-born aetheriest?"

"Maybe." Kro folded his arms. "It's enviable, since you get to skip a lot of basic training, but one fluctuation in your emotions could be extremely dangerous. For example, if your temper got out of control, you could compress the air around someone's head and make them explode with just a look."

Mekial's face dropped and he looked at his friends. They were just as alarmed.

"That's why an innate still needs training," Kro said. "And the more I think about what you told me about all that's happened to you, the more sense it makes…"

"Are innate aetheriests common?" Mekial asked nervously.

"No. They're extremely rare. The Aether Academy in the imperial capital prides itself on recruiting them, whenever they are found, and puts them on the fast-track for military enlistment. I don't even think Heldar's ever met one."

"What can an innate aetheriest do that makes them so special?"

Dillon asked.

"For one thing they're born with an abnormally high concentration of quintessence," Kro answered. "A small fluctuation in their emotions, whether it's caused by shock or excitement, can link them to the aether. Once they get the hang of what's inside them, their influence is also insane. And, I've heard that once their quintessence reaches a certain level, their eyes actually change color. It's said to be a sort of greenish-blue, which some think might be the color of the aether itself. But, that in and of itself isn't even common among innates. The aether's still a powerful thing to connect to, and the amount of exposure to the aether that you'd need in order to reach that state is demanding."

"Wow!" Lilian exclaimed, absolutely thrilled. "Innates must be the strongest aetheriests in the whole world!"

Kro chuckled. "You'd think so. But there's actually an aetheriest that's stronger than an innate."

"Really?" Mekial frowned, almost offended. "What?"

"An aetherian," Kro answered, a gleam in his eye.

"Like Zion the Hero?!" Dillon burst excitedly.

"And Moriji, who fought a whole army by herself in the Nassaulean plains!" Lilian added.

"That was so cool!" Kurt agreed enthusiastically.

"Right…" Kro smiled weakly, for the characters that they'd mentioned were only fictional. "I admit, those are some pretty good examples of what aetherians can pull off. In the world of aetheriests, they're the strongest ones out there. Supposedly, once an innate reaches the point where their eyes change color, they're not too far off from becoming an aetherian themselves. But that's rare." He waved the idea way. "Becoming an aetherian isn't exactly common. I don't think there's been one for centuries…"

"Whoa…" Dillon looked at Mekial, as did the others.

"You could be a natural-born aetheriest!" Lilian grabbed his hand and jumped up and down. "And then, you could become an *aetherian!* And kick slave traders' butts!"

"Yeah…" Though Lilian's idea would've energized him on most days, Mekial's face became rather distant in response. "I've always been able to do weird stuff since I was really little, and even weirder things have been happening in the last few years. There's the thing with the entelodon. And you know, before that, I ripped my dad's laundry with a sneeze while they were drying, and I knocked Ren's sword off her wall without even touching it! I think."

"Those sound like happy accidents." Klarys frowned.

"No they're not!" Mekial retorted and he turned on Kro. "I'm gonna figure this out once and for all, no matter how long it takes!"

"All right then." Kro rested a fist on his side. His smile was one of determination. "Let's get started."

"You bet!"

59

WITH A SOUNDLESS flash of winking flesh, Adiné blinked her troubled, dark eyes.

The Avat slaves who'd hung the painting against the red and gold walls awaited her verdict. The work depicted a woman, one with beautiful eyes of black and deep burgundy hair that rested on her shoulders in thick waves. Her soft brown face was touched with a gentle smile, pleasant, and her kind stare was full of a compassion that Adiné would never know, and thus would never receive.

She wondered what her life would've been like if things were different.

She blinked again. "Move the left side higher."

Obediently, the Avat servants turned upon their wooden step stools and tilted the angle of the hand-carved frame.

At last, it was straight.

But off-center.

Adiné's thin, shapely eyebrows furrowed in disappointment.

A knock came from the door behind her.

"Enter," she replied without turning.

The study's door clicked open. "Begging your pardon, Your Highness," came the voice of the man who'd arrived.

"Oh." Adiné circled a bit, the clenching in her chest unwinding just a little. "Mattatheus. Come in."

The man entered the room fully. Leaving the parlor's door open behind him, he crossed the mosaic floor to stand beside the princess.

He was Mattatheus, a young and handsome Arkanian with olive skin and short black hair that touched his brow. His oceanic eyes, glinting beneath thick eyebrows, were as striking as his chiseled jaw, creating such a complementary set of features that any sculptor in the Empire would gush over the chance at preserving him in marble. Even his form was picturesque, for he was tall and broad-shouldered, and his natural physique offered him a certain level of authority over others.

It was a convenient blessing — after all, he was appointed to become Princess Adiné's aide for when she became the viceroy in her father's stead. At that point, his political position and command would be second only to hers.

But that was for a later time. At present he acted as her tutor in history and political affairs, even though he was only four years older than she, and he possessed a knowledge that spanned the continent's imperial history, from its birth to its present.

While the princess appreciated her father's recruitment of him, she couldn't help but feel that Mattatheus was also commissioned as her bodyguard and nanny. If she stayed in one place for too long, he almost always managed to sniff her out. After that, he wouldn't let her out of his sight. Needless to say, she wasn't particularly fond of his company.

But at that moment, she didn't mind it.

Dressed in a dark blue tunic and overchest corset, a black cape, and double-belted trousers tucked into his boots, he scrutinized the painting for a moment. Against the red and black fresco walls and Arkanian decorum, and even compared to the slaves, he was stunning, as were his clothes, for unlike the popular dress of the Empire he often went about in noble wear that was more familiar to certain historic families of his hometown: Barrae. Given his own lineage as a descendant of the lords who'd forged a treaty with Axelius Arkania when he'd expanded into their lands, it was no wonder.

"So, it's finished," he deduced. He planted a hand on his side. "It looks good. Navareus has outdone himself."

"I suppose he did. But, I can't help but wonder if it really is her." Adiné's once harsh and analytical stare softened with uncertainty. "This painting arrived earlier today. I know Navareus is the best painter in all of Arkania, but I don't remember what my mother looked like. So far, aside from the family portrait that he made for us, this is all I have to go on. But, I can't help but wonder if it's only what he *thinks* she looked like."

Mattatheus looked at her.

Adiné had set her sad eyes on the floor. Her hands, usually laced neatly over the front of her flowing dress, were tightened. He could see the delicate outline of bones showing through her skin.

"I've only met Her Highness a few times, before Viceroy Diomedes appointed me as your future aide." Mattatheus looked upon the painting again. "From what I can remember, it looks just like her. Don't worry." He smiled gently at Adiné. "A better artist couldn't have been picked. I'm sure the viceroy knew that himself."

Adiné lifted sorrowful eyes to the image once more. "I hope so."

"Is this all right, then, Your Highness?" one of the servants ventured to ask from one of the ladders.

"Do you need it adjusted more?" the other continued.

"O-oh. No. It's fine." Adiné smiled thinly. "I'm sorry for keeping you. You may go now."

"Yes, Princess." The both of them bowed their heads, climbed down the step stools, and departed with them.

Mattatheus turned back to Adiné after they'd gone. The first thing he noticed was that her hands were no longer clenched together.

"Do they still frighten you?" he asked. "The Avat people."

Adiné looked at him quickly and then away. "...Is it that obvious?"

"You're always reserved when they're around. It doesn't exactly suit you."

"I can't help it." Adiné scowled at nothing. "I hear of them leading insurrections all over the place these days. Just a few weeks ago there was one in Almstead and another near the mines by Cleopa. And then, there was Orinn..."

Mattatheus' eyes inched away. "They're a dissatisfied people. That much is certain."

Adiné looked at him.

He didn't meet her gaze this time. "They're at the bottom of the food chain, so to speak. Even I can't blame them for being angry over their situation, and retaliating."

Adiné looked down again, distressed.

"But that doesn't mean it should frighten you, Miss."

Their eyes met.

"The Empire of Arkania has held this continent for over four hundred years," he reminded her. "And the Avat people have been our slaves from the beginning. They could try to war against us for the rest of time — it wouldn't change anything. And you have no reason to fear them attacking you here." He glanced at the soldiers who were stationed on either side of the parlor, as stiff as statues, nearly looking to be a part of the decorations.

"Yeah." Adiné laid eyes on her smiling mother again. Then, she found the woman's name, which had been chiseled into a gold plaque at the bottom of the image: Valis. "I guess you're right."*tv*

⤚ ✣ ⤛

Legs crossed and eyes closed, Mekial sat on the bank of the river.

Around him Lilian, Dillon, Lacey, Klarys and Kurt watched the water intensely. Kurt gulped.

At their backs Kro was just as attentive, arms folded, brow furrowed.

Suddenly, Lilian threw her head back with an exasperated groan. "Kro! He's been doing this all day! When is he gonna be done?!"

"When he actually does it!" was the vexed response.

It was Mekial's turn to growl in frustration and his eyes popped open. "I can't concentrate. There's too much noise!"

Kro bowed his head with a sigh of disappointment.

"That's because we're near the *waterfalls!*" Lilian gestured to them impatiently. "They're noisy!"

FEAR NOTHING
CODE: INSECURITY

"If you wanted quiet, maybe you guys should've picked like…I dunno, that lake in Heletia Cavern or something," Dillon suggested. "Or even the one in the valley!"

"But Kro just said I might have abnormally high quintessence, and the only way to find out is if I'm able to counteract the flow of incredibly turbulent water!" Mekial pouted and planted an elbow into his leg while clapping his chin in his hand. He glared at the disobedient river.

"What does that even mean?" Lilian wrinkled her nose.

"I think it means he has to make this so-called aether training as hard as possible," Dillon translated wisely.

"Yeah!" Mekial sat up and clapped his hands around his knees. "The water in Heletia's lake is way too calm, and so's the one in the valley."

"But wouldn't it have been easier to find out if you were an aetheriest by trying to influence calm water instead of water that's already moving everywhere?" Klarys asked smartly.

Mekial just sulked.

"You know I'm right."

"Be quiet!"

"Calm water could've worked," Kro added in, coming forward. "But if Mekial is an innate, it shouldn't matter what state the water's in. It'd respond to him."

"We've been out here for a really long time," Lacey whined, sitting on her bottom and pressing her hands into the dirt. "And we didn't bring a lot of food with us. I'm really hungry!"

"Fine, you guys can go home." Mekial frowned at the tearing water.

"Mek, we missed classes with Miss Yulia at the schoolhouse *and* you skipped your training with Jeffrey!" Dillon reminded him.

"If you get back too late you're not gonna be able to wake up in time for training tomorrow," Kurt added worriedly, "and then Jeffrey'll make you do twice as much stuff to make up for missing two lessons. I bet Miss Yulia's already thinking to punish all of us for missing hers!"

"I know, I know…" Mekial's frown faded. "But I just…I really wanna figure this out. That entelodon should've broken all my ribs or something." A sparkle entered his eye. "Unless I've just got rock-hard abs."

Kro rubbed his forehead.

Klarys rolled her eyes.

"And then you woke up," Dillon said.

"I could have rock-hard abs!"

"They seem pretty squishy to me." Lilian poked his stomach.

"Stop that!" He twisted away.

"Well, there's always tomorrow." Kro shrugged nonchalantly. "I should probably get back to my patrol, anyway."

"Yeah, and I wanna eat." Lacey rubbed her stomach.

Lilian dropped into the dirt next to her. "I'm really hungry, too. If I don't eat soon, I'm gonna be mad at all of you."

"Why?" Klarys frowned at her.

"Cuz I get really mad when I'm hungry! Uncle Liam says I shouldn't let my emotions control me like that," she recalled regretfully, "but I can't help it! So, sorry ahead if I start hurting people's feelings."

"Appreciate the honesty." Klarys thought about it for a second. "I guess."

"I said you guys can go if you want to," Mekial said again, twisting to look at them.

"We can't just leave you here!" Klarys argued. "This is…" She glanced around and then dropped her voice to a whisper. *"The Empire."*

"I'll be fine." Mekial pointed at Kro. "If anything does go wrong, Kro'll help me out!"

"Way to volunteer me," Kro said, then he sighed theatrically. "But, if I must."

"I also grabbed this!" Mekial dug into the satchel he was wearing and proudly pulled out a black pole that was just about a foot long.

Kro frowned at it. "The heck's that?"

Klarys' concerned look instantly morphed into a puzzled frown, and she took it from him. It wasn't heavy, but it glinted like metal when she held it up to the sun.

"Me and the other trainees got to see a bunch of new stuff

that the engineers are working on," Mekial explained to Kro. "It's supposed to be a new tool for the raiders. It kinda looks like one of those smoke bombs, but instead it can be used as a distress signal, or as a distraction on raids. Or something."

"Oh." Kro crossed his arms. "Right, I heard they were developing that. For missions where the teams are short on aetheriests. We can send off our own distress signals."

"How does it work?" Kurt took the strange object next. He tried looking through it like a telescope and frowned with disappointment when he learned it had no eyehole.

"It shoots light into the air or…something. But it's a prototype so be careful with it!" Mekial added at a hasty shout and he snatched it from Kurt before the boy could pop off its bottom piece.

"You swiped that from the engineers' shop?" Dillon asked, reaching for it.

"Yes!" Mekial pulled it away before Dillon could touch it and he stuffed it back into his bag.

Dillon's bothered look fizzed out with realization. "But if it's a prototype, no one back home'll recognize it."

"The engineers will!" Mekial protested. "Besides, there was nothing else to grab that would've worked the same."

"Who'da thunk that the rule-abiding Mekial would rob the engineers?" Klarys asked, her voice sharp with mockery.

Mekial fought off his guilt. "Well, I can't go into the Empire unprepared! Even if I am an aetheriest."

Klarys' eyelids dropped halfway. "You can only be an aetheriest if you've been trained! You've been training, and nothing's happening. We should just go home!"

"You don't know that for sure! Kro just said it himself!" He pointed at the older villager. "I could be a *prodigy!*"

"No you're not! You're not an aetheriest!"

"You don't know that!"

Lacey giggled. "Looks like you're not the only one who gets cranky when they're hungry, Lil."

Lilian smiled. "At least I won't have to worry about being the only one who hurts people's feelings!"

"Hey!" Dillon cried. "I think something happened to the water!"

Mekial got excited. "Really? What?"

"I don't know, it like, bubbled or something!"

His interest piquing, Kro looked over in Dillon's direction.

"Sure it wasn't a fish?" Klarys asked.

"I dunno…" Dillon scratched his head. "I think it happened when Mek got mad."

"Quick, Klarys, make him mad again!" Kurt encouraged.

"You're not an aetheriest, you're not an aetheriest," Klarys teased in a sing-song voice while poking Mekial's forehead.

"Stop that!" He smacked her hand away.

A part of the river bubbled like it was being heated from below.

"Stop!" Kro swung his arm out, and the children altogether stopped.

The river returned to its naturally turbulent state.

Kro slowly turned to Mekial, who was staring at the water. As if he could feel Kro's eyes on him, he faced him.

Behind them, Lacey suddenly stiffened and looked around. She stood up quickly.

Lilian noticed. "What's wrong?" she asked.

"I thought I heard something." Lacey turned to face the trees that stood behind them, then studied the entire wood that enclosed the river.

Dillon moved next to her and listened for a moment. "…I don't hear anything."

"That's cuz you're a half-Avat, like me!" Lilian piped up. "Uncle Liam says that full-blooded Avats can hear better than us. If Lacey said something's coming, then I believe her."

"Is it someone from Taranis?" Kurt asked, coming near. "Can you tell?"

"Mm…" Lacey frowned, straining her pointy ears for any other noises. "I can't…"

Kro's forehead slowly creased with mounting concern, and he cast his gaze across the opposite shore.

Lacey took off her hood and pushed back the tunic she wore on her head, revealing her sharp ears.

"Lacey!" Klarys exclaimed.

Lacey ignored her, her hands cupped around her ears and her eyes closed. "It…sounds like metal." She opened her eyes with a steep frown. "Metal…feet? And voices…"

Dillon's gaze wandered away as she spoke, treading through the trees near them to snag onto a distant flash of movement.

The faint sound of men shouting at one another mounted in his ears at the same time, mingling with the roar of the falls in such a way that he nearly dismissed them as his imagination.

But then another roar came, louder than the tumbling water and howling towards them faster than a cannonball.

Kro couldn't hear it.

But he could sense it.

"Look out!" he yelled, his voice joined by Dillon's and Lacey's, and together they shoved their group into the trees before a wave of fire bombed across the riverbank, tearing up foliage and undergrowth with a monstrous bellow.

Scrambling to their feet, they sought shelter a good distance away and stole a look back.

A towering wall of fire met their eyes, masking the river behind a dancing curtain of flames that soared above the trees.

Kurt caught his breath first. "Where'd that even come from?!" he cried.

"Cut it out, Mekial!" Klarys snapped, rounding on him. "If you could use the aether this whole time, you don't have to scare us with it!"

"It's not me!" Mekial glared at her, only to lose confidence a second later. "At least, I don't think it is —"

"Take that south bend! You men, this way!"

"Check by that trail, there's a hollow through those trees!"

"Get down!" Kro hissed, falling to his knees as the unfamiliar voices continued.

As the children dropped around him, he crept towards the edge of a hill close by and peeked over it.

Several men were dashing by below, their armor gleaming in the mottled sunlight. Armored collars that were linked to plated shoulder guards framed their upper bodies, and underneath this protection they wore padded purple tunics that were emblazoned with a golden emblem on their chests. Gauntlets that were hinged to flexible metal gloves concealed their forearms and fingertips, and across their waists they wore belts from which hung a single, uniform broadsword. Shields were strapped to their backs.

In watching them, Kro soon caught a good glimpse of the emblem that was on their chests, which he identified as an image of Empyrean. On either side of its spread wings and upturned beak, there were two Arkanian letters.

He translated them into the words that they represented, having only known to do so thanks to the stories that he'd heard from intelligence scouts.

Just our luck.

When his olive eyes turned to the children, they were stern. "Don't move."

Turning back around, he hopped over the hill and skidded to the level below.

Lacey squeaked with fright, but Klarys quickly covered her mouth and pulled her back.

"You there!" One of the imperials stopped in mid-run, spying Kro just as he came from around a tree.

Kro pointed at himself innocently. "Who, me?"

"An order has been issued to the neighboring towns, declaring Odelwhite Forest off-limits to civilians." The soldier looked upon his fellow Arkanian with a suspicious eye. Around him, the rest of his unit disappeared along the road up ahead. "Why are you here?"

"Wow, seriously? I must've missed the memo!" Kro waved his hands defensively, all while keeping a smile on his face. "I come here pretty early for my daily exercises. Y'know, sprint through the hills, grab a tree branch, do some chin-ups."

The imperial grunted.

As the two conversed, Mekial crawled on his belly to find out what was happening. He squinted at the soldier's armor for a second, analyzing it.

At last he twisted to the others, his eyes large, and he whispered his finding. *"It's Empyrean's Guard!"*

The color drained from their faces.

Suddenly, Lacey yelped and hid behind Klarys.

Dillon and Lilian tensed, catching the same sound that Lacey had, and as one the group turned to see another guardsman step through the trees near them.

Spotting them, the soldier blinked in surprise. "What the…?"

"Odelwhite Forest is too dangerous for civilians to be in right now," the guardsman before Kro reiterated. "I must ask for you to come with me. I will escort you safely to the border. From there on, please return home on your own."

"Why's it off-limits?" Kro asked, still keeping to that blameless persona.

"Reports suggest that some of the savages and devils who terrorize the Empire are located in these woods," the man answered. "We're here to eradicate them."

Kro's façade nearly slipped. "Eradicate?"

Behind him, Lacey screamed.

He whirled. "Lacey —!"

In the exact same moment, the guardsman who'd stumbled upon the children noticed Lacey's ears, as well as the unquestionable attire that she and the other children were wearing beneath their haphazard disguises.

"Hey!" he hollered to the man Kro was speaking with. "I found some goblins and savages! They're here!"

"You know what to do," said the other.

"Sir!" His subordinate drew his blade.

Kro's eyes sharpened into daggers and he joined the aether. Hardening his stance, he flexed his arms and twisted at the hip.

Before the children's eyes, the ground beneath the guardsman sank and spun him in an isolated circle. Then, it fired him into the air like a springboard.

Before the other imperial could react to what he'd done Kro waved his arms, calling up a tree root.

The creaking branch coiled into the air and surrounded the imperial like a basilisk. Winding itself back, it hurled him through the canopy and out of sight.

"You guys okay?!" Kro shouted up at the children, dropping his stance.

"Yeah, we're good!" Dillon called back, poking his head into Kro's view. "Thank you!"

Kro's urgent expression softened with relief.

"Over here!"

Kro turned, his cloak flapping loudly.

A guardsman had returned. Clearly, he'd seen what had happened.

"Savages!" he shouted, likely to alert any other guardsmen in the area. "They're over here!"

He changed his footing and within seconds, the aether touched Kro's skin.

But it was more apparent than what he was used to.

Eyes growing in understanding, Kro spread his own feet.

A blast of wind erupted around him, and the same green-blue light that the children had witnessed before descended around his body. *"Get down!"* he roared.

Dillon ducked out of view, and he and his friends huddled together.

The imperial aetheriest lifted his hand.

Responding to his influence the aether granted him a flame that danced wildly, shone brightly. Once it had reached the size that the imperial wanted, he sent it surging in Kro's direction.

With a violent roar the fire blazed towards the villager, bombing through trees and bushes like a radioactive missile.

Kro stretched his hands out and a blast of mist left them. It swirled upward quickly, curving around him like an apparition before it hardened into a clear wall of protection.

Howling terribly, the flames slammed into it like an avalanche.

Fire went everywhere and Kro cried out, his arms and knees buckling. Cracks splintered through his barrier like knotted spider-webs.

"Kro!" Mekial yelled, his hair swaying in the hot air.

Kro winced, his arms shaking. Through the fires that danced outside of his shield, he watched as the imperial aetheriest stretched out his hand again.

This time the fire that he made remained close to his fingers, enveloping them. Gradually they encircled his hand, his wrist, his arm, and then they moved to encase his entire body.

Kro's eyes grew large and his stomach dropped. When he spoke, his voice was hardly louder than the roaring fires and crackling timber. "No way."

"Kro!" Mekial hollered again. "Are you okay?!"

"Mekial!" Kro shouted warningly —

— the imperial aetheriest was completely hidden by a wall of flames now, and the fire was growing fast —

"RUN!"

When the guardsman next struck Kro's shield, the resulting explosion sent a cloud of smoke ballooning into the sky.

～ ✄ ～

"…I mean, it stunk so bad it coulda knocked a buzzard off a gut wagon!" Eklaire plugged her nose as she shared her anecdote with Brent. The two had finished picking prunes, and were sitting in the clearing with their fruit basket leaning against Eklaire's legs. "When I finally asked what he was makin', the ol' coot had the nerve to say, 'Dinner!'"

Brent laughed. "That's why your house smelled like that for the next three days?"

"Yeah! Pa kept havin' us open the windows, but then people'd complain that the smell was gettin' out! I'm just glad Harver talked Jeffrey into lettin' us crash on over at their place for a bit, while one of her doohickeys cleared out the air at ours. But it was awful! Stench was caught in my nose'n I couldn't eat nothin' for *days*. I got so hungry, it felt like my stomach was chewin' my backbone!"

Brent laughed harder, tears in his eyes. "And this whole time everyone kept thinking something died under your house…but you guys just fell victim to Elder Atkin's cooking!"

"He's a real sweet ol' man, bless his heart," Eklaire sighed, sitting back on her hands. "But that food was somethin' else! Coulda gagged a maggot, let me tell ya!"

As the two continued to chat Aaron remained at the edge of the orchard, idly carving a stray piece of bark with his hunting knife. He glanced up with a distracted frown, thinking he'd heard something in the distance, only to do a double-take at the sight of the horizon.

He stood up. "Hey…Brent!"

Behind him Brent turned from sharing his own story, and Eklaire quieted her laughter.

Aaron wasn't looking at them. Instead he had his eyes fixed on something that was over the valley — something that appeared to lie in the direction of Taranis.

"You should come see this," he said.

Brent's eyebrows creased questioningly. Standing, he jogged to Aaron's side and upon arriving there, he followed the redhead's line of sight.

His eyes narrowed.

Thanks to the plateau's elevation they could see over the whole valley, from the trees that crowned Taranis' hilltop to the mountains that bordered the Empire. Beyond those peaks, the emerald sea of Odelwhite Forest was just as visible —

And so was the massive cloud of smoke that was swelling out of it.

Eklaire ran to join them, basket in hand, and she skittered to a halt when she saw what had rendered them so silent. "I-is that… some kinda wildfire?"

"No…" Brent didn't face her. "We don't get wildfires."

⚜

From a lip of land that protruded out of a mountainside, Saruke's Shade squatted down and looked out over Odelwhite Forest.

Smoke was billowing through its luscious canopy to haze the air, and flames lashed between the burning trees. So far, the spreading flames were isolated to the Revere Falls region, but he was almost certain that if things continued, the destruction would spread along the mountains that ringed the forest.

That was probably what Empyrean's Guard wanted.

"Hmm…" He drummed his fingers against the side of his mask.

"Are we too late?" a young woman behind him asked.

It was Kyrah, a young scout and aetheriest of Taranis.

"No." The masked warrior stood, and the heated wind from below picked up his mane and tossed it about.

It didn't ignore the ragtag group of runaways and mercenaries that were behind him — nor did it pass over the intelligence scouts that Taranis had considered missing, including Kyrah.

With his shrouded eyes lingering on the growing fires below, Saruke's Shade rested a hand on the hilt of his sword. "I'm never late."

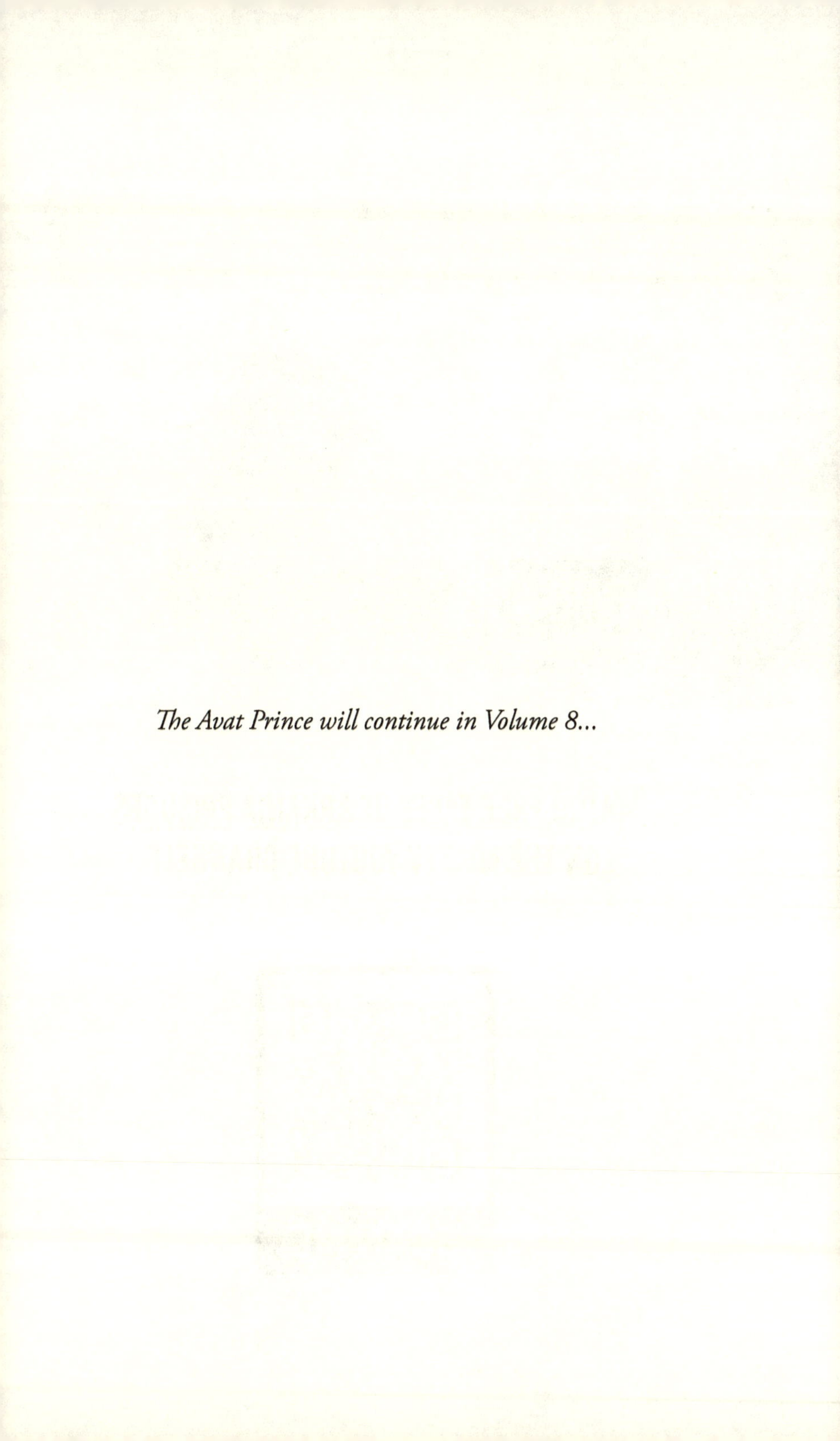

The Avat Prince will continue in Volume 8...

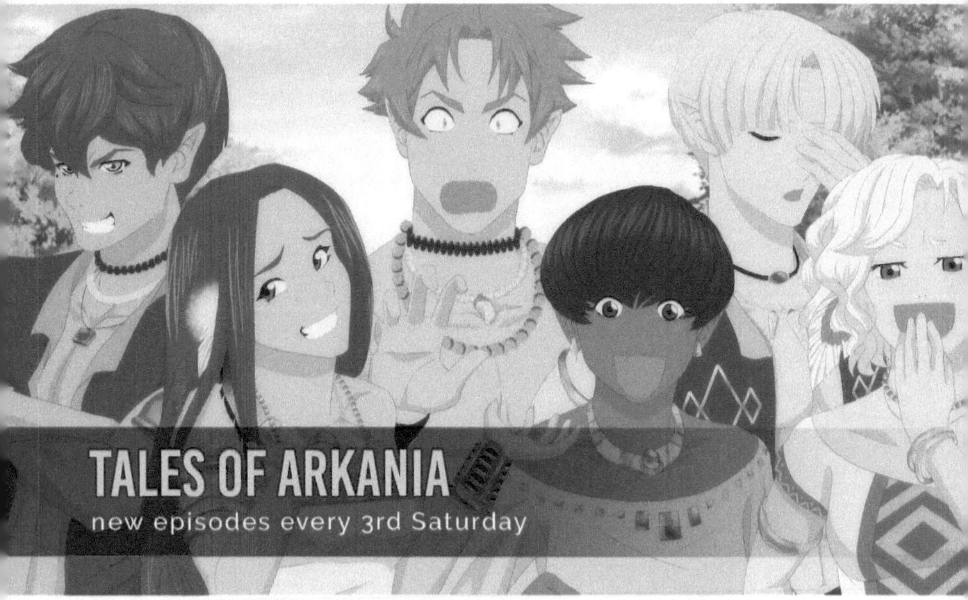

WATCH <u>FREE TALES OF ARKANIA EPISODES</u> ON THE MVP TV YOUTUBE CHANNEL!

NEW THRILLS. NEW TALES.

Brand-new bonus content for *The Avat Prince* every third Saturday!

Featuring an international cast of voice talent, including award-winning VA Josh Portillo!

DON'T FORGET TO LIKE AND SUBSCRIBE!
AND TURN THE PAGE TO PREVIEW VOL. 8!

THE AVAT PRINCE: VOLUME 8

ILLON'S HEART RATE spiked when he caught the sound of an approach. His head snapped up.

A trio of guardsmen had found them and after taking a short survey of the young villagers, the one in the middle spoke up. "Take the goblins to the camp," he said darkly. "As for the savages…" He gave Mekial, Klarys and the unconscious Kurt a once-over, likely pausing to consider their youth. He dismissed it. "We don't need them."

Silently his men advanced, hands going for their swords.

The children huddled nearer to one another.

Dillon leaned over Kurt protectively.

At the front of the group, Mekial dropped a hand to where his knives were and groped for their handles. But they weren't there.

It took him a split second to remember why. Even so, he widened his stance before his friends.

No sooner had he taken this position did a black-clad figure leap out from behind a tree near the commanding guardsman. A flash of silver showed that his sword was already drawn.

In the blink of an eye he was behind the imperial, one hand latching around his chin to point his face towards the sky and expose his neck. Flicking his blade out and over the vulnerable area, the warrior slashed his sword across it and flung the man's body away, then turned his masked face to the guardsmen who remained.

Overcoming their surprise for his sudden assault, they launched at him with their swords out.

The warrior easily deflected their strikes, creating a clang of metal that sang a furious duet with the crackling forest. He was lithe, nimble, and despite the fact that he was facing elite members of the Empire's forces — outnumbered, no less — he held his own.

Blocking one of the guardsmen's attacks with an upward stroke, he cut across his neck with a second swing, killing him. Turning on the other, he struck him with a kick so ferocious that the man actually spiraled and smashed into a tree face-first. Without a sound, he sank against it.

The warrior turned on the children next. It was then they realized that he was wearing a mask.

With its horrible fangs drawn into a cheek-high grin, it seemed to be aware of some heinous punchline that no one else had heard, and a wild mane of hair framed its lion-like face. But its most prominent feature was on its brow.

Painted there was the Liberation Fronts' insignia of encircling and partly disconnected rings.

Mekial frowned.

Quaking with a fear that she desperately tried to hide, Klarys hid Lacey behind her.

Lilian inched behind Mekial.

Dillon continued to cover Kurt.

The man said nothing. It was like he was frozen as he watched them, studied them.

Then, with his bloody sword at his side, he marched towards them, his frightening face silhouetted against the flames that lashed in the distance.

Mekial's knees buckled in preparation of a fight, and he fought to find his voice. It shook out of his throat before he managed to even it out. "Leave us alone!"

The man stopped.

Mekial hid his shock and remained in that protective stance in front of his friends. He tried to sound strong in spite of the terror pounding through him. "Who are you?"

The swordsman didn't reply. The only thing he did was swipe

his sword to the side, spattering the ground with gore. It was then that the children noticed the blade.

It was of Avat craftsmanship.

Mekial spoke up again. "Well?"

Crackling flames filled in for the man's silence. At long last, he replied.

"It's a long walk back to Taranis." His voice sounded just as sinister as his mask looked. "If you want to make it home, you'd better stick with me."

**CONTINUE READING IN
THE AVAT PRINCE: VOLUME 8!**

About the Author(ess)

Myranda V. Peterson

A young artist who wears many hats, Myranda Victoria Peterson is an author, illustrator, animator and voice director with a contagious passion for storytelling. She first started off writing plays, which her parents and friends helped her perform when she was a little girl. A self-taught artist, her creative work is heavily inspired by anime and Japanese pop culture. She creates original, high-fantasy content that aims to inspire the youth of today with themes of generosity, courage, friendship and hope.

Myranda is the founder and CEO of the independent imprint and joint animation studio House MVP and lives in Boston, where many famous, classic authors have gone before her. She hopes that one day, her name will join them!